Yes, Chef! And Other Stories

Nykky Roadarmel

Copyright 2024 Nykky Roadarmel

Cover art and layout by Rooster Republic Press

Edited by Lyndsey Smith at Horrorsmith Editing

This is a work of fiction. Unless otherwise indicated, all the names, characters, businesses, places, events and incidents in this book are either the product of the author's imagination or used in a fictitious manner. Any resemblance to actual persons, living or dead, or actual events is purely coincidental.

No part of this book may be reproduced, stored in a retrieval system, or transmitted in any form or by any means, without the prior permission in writing of the author, nor be otherwise circulated in any form of binding or cover than that in which it is published and without a similar condition including this condition being imposed on the subsequent purchaser.

For Nikolaus

"You're the best!
Around!
Nothing's gonna ever keep you down!"

A special thanks to the indie author community on Facebook. There's
too many of you to name, but I hope you all know who you are.
You all have motivated, inspired, and supported me—more than most
people I know in "real life."
The help, suggestions, honesty, and humor you provide
is something I treasure.
Don't ever change.
Keep writing.

"...Members of families who eat together regularly are statistically less likely to stick up liquor stores, blow up meth labs, give birth to crack babies, commit suicide, or make donkey porn. If Little Timmy just had more meatloaf, he might not have grown up to fill chest freezers with Cub Scout parts."
-Anthony Bourdain

Contents

Wolf Road is a Death Trap

S heila Buckman knew what she had to do, and there was almost no time to get it done. She stared at the street sign from about ten feet back. Decrepit, covered with dust from the last storm...she was surprised it still stood. That sign would always be there however—both a warning and an invitation.

Sheila gripped the wheel as tight as she could and began to sweat. Her heart had basically pounded out of her chest by this point, but she could do nothing until Ned called with the confirmation. Clovis was secure in the front seat, watching Sheila try to hide her nerves and hesitation.

She began to think of a time before the world had dried up. Before people started changing and the sky became orange. The sun was almost visible today, too. Sheila wondered when the sun was going to finally die and rid the planet of the leftover filth.

Her thoughts were interrupted by a gust of wind covering the windshield with a blanket of dust and dirt. This was the closest to the road Sheila had ever been. The black of night hid her from *Them*—and whatever else was out there.

Ned had told her to stay there with the engine off and wait for his call on the talker. It was amazing those pieces of junk still worked. Even more amazing she had been able to rebuild this truck. Risking her life for Clovis was not what she had in mind, but the truck and this plan might just make it all feasible.

"*Sheilds. You there?*"

Sheila looked at the talker. *This is it*, she thought. *No fucking turning back now.*

"Ned."

"*You have about sixty seconds before the second shift ends. How is our boy?*"

"He's quiet right now. I think he's more ready than I am. The doc there?" Sheila tried to stop her voice from trembling.

"*Yes,*" Ned said. "*We're ready for you. When you get to the end, take a right. You won't miss us.*"

"All right. Well, here goes nothing."

"*Sixty seconds are up! Go!*" Ned yelled.

Sheila started the engine, shifted into first gear, and floored it, squealing right on to Wolf Road.

Only about three miles of this shit. I can do this. I can do this!

Sheila shifted to next gear and flicked on the fog lights. They revealed body after body—some fresh, some only skeletal remains. There was no point in avoiding them at the speed she was going, but Sheila tried.

More dust tornadoed through the air from the truck tires and it would not settle. Then one of *Them* came at her on the right.

"HOLD ON CLOVIS!" Sheila jerked the wheel to the left, gaining enough traction for *It* to fall to the ground. She stopped the truck.

Bright red eyes, black teeth, and black talons.

It looked directly at her through the rearview mirror, then ate tail pipe when Sheila backed over *It*. She would have pulled forward and reversed over *It* again, but there was no time. Sheila took half a second to confirm the kill, shifted into gear, and kept going.

Two more were coming. Two sets of eyes in the air this time, and they were flying full force toward her windshield. Sheila hadn't planned on using the mini-gun mounted to the top of the truck this early in because more noise meant more of them.

"Well shit." She quickly flipped open the lever on the dash and pressed the button under it, hoping for the best. The shots were almost deafening, and Sheila was more worried about Clovis's little ears than anything else.

Thunk! She got one of *Them!*

The wipers took care of the blood and other parts raining down on her vehicle.

Sheila felt the whoosh of the second. She turned off the gun and floored the gas as hard as she could. The dust was making it more and more difficult to see, and suddenly the road became uneven.

Should I slow down? Sheila thought she must be halfway at this point.

But there was a horde. Twenty? Fifty? One hundred? It was unclear because of the dark, the dirt, and the multiple fresh ones flocking to the truck. Sheila hit as many as she could without bottoming out. These ones were just trekkers—fast as hell, but no wings yet.

Clovis started whining and fidgeting in the seat.

"It's okay, baby! It's okay!" Sheila rammed the clutch, changed gears, and switched up another lever.

Blades released from all sides of the truck, piercing legs and torsos, blood spraying everywhere. The mirrors turned crimson, and the windshield wipers could hardly keep up. Ned had warned her she might have to stop if she used the "sword-guns," as he so eloquently nick-named them. They had been his idea.

Sheila pummeled through the rest of the horde, checking the rearview for the flying one that got away. Glass suddenly shattered to her left, exploding on her face.

"Fuck!"

One of *Them* had been impaled by a sword-gun and was stuck to her truck like a fly on shit. The bars she had installed kept *Its* greasy fingers from getting through the window but it was only a matter of time.

It's now or never. Or dead.

Sheila slammed on the brakes, grabbed the hand-cannon from her boot and pointed it at the creature through the broken window. More blood sprayed her truck making it look like a macabre vehicle of death. The blades weren't retracting like they should. Probably because whatever had been left of *Its* body was blocking them from turning inward.

Sheila shushed Clovis and quickly got out of the truck. Using her buck knife, she wielded what was left of the creature's body from the blade. "Goodbye, you fuck." Her victory was short-lived when the sound of the flapping wings came toward her.

Nope. This can't be it. We don't die today.

Sheila hopped back in, Clovis whined as loud as he ever had. She hesitated, then punched the truck in reverse. The flying one soared just past her. Sheila, Clovis, and the truck stood idle during the silent battle. *It* knew about the mini gun because she had killed the creature's friend right in front of *It*.

It looked straight in her eyes while an even bigger horde was making its way toward them all. Broken pavement, a flying monster, the dead, and who knew what else, were keeping Sheila from getting to the end of Wolf Road.

She gripped the stick-shift and looked at Clovis. His beautiful, reflective green eyes though sad-looking, gave her the reassurance she needed.

"We don't die today!" Sheila yelled her battle cry, popped the truck into gear and floored it. The mini-gun spewed everything it had left. She screamed as each abnormal leg and arm exploded into the night. The truck bounced and fishtailed, and blood and dust swirled around them, like a hurricane of nightmares and body parts.

Well past the point of no return, the end of the street became visible. The number of bodies seemed to dissipate the closer Sheila got. The ammo reader read "0" in a disturbing, bright red—like those alarm clocks she used to see before the world went straight to shit. Sheila saw the street sign at the end of the road and prepared to take that right turn, just as Ned had instructed, but she slammed on the brakes.

That flying bastard still isn't dead.

It got closer. A wounded wing and broken claws. It wasn't giving up—but neither was Sheila.

On the corner of Wolf and whatever street was going to bring her and Clovis home free, Sheila reached behind her seat, grabbing the "Just in Case" bag. It was heavy, but it was necessary at this point.

She unzipped it, grabbed the large, metal cylinder, and exited the truck.

Sheila had one chance. If there was only one shot in the entire universe that mattered, this was it. And she knew it.

Though the creature was wounded, *It* was gaining momentum. Sheila adjusted the shoulder-stop and removed the safety pin. She moved the sights forward and balanced out the muzzle covers, then dis-engaged the cocking lever. Pressing the third and final safety mechanism, Sheila aimed and pulled the trigger, perfectly hitting *It* in the chest,

It exploded, slamming to the ground and spitting up dust becoming a puddle of blood.

"Yes!" Sheila floored it to the next street, where hundreds of bright road flares lit her path.

"Sheilds!" Ned yelled, grabbing the carrier from the front seat of Sheila's truck.

Sheila was dirty, bloody, and ready for the doctor, who stood next to Ned, to help Clovis.

Stumbling from the truck, she looked at the doctor. "So. You're the last veterinarian on the planet?"

"And you're the last person willing to die for your cat?"

"Die? Not today."

The Gnawing

A fter the sudden death of his mother, Mike Brubacher found himself in the attic of his childhood home. He had known this day would come and after the thirtieth or so rejection of his manuscript, figured time away from his failed writing could be some sort of recharge/make-peace-with-grief moment.

Unfortunately, his mother had held on to everything. Fortunately, her compulsive tendencies also came with organization. As many boxes, totes, and bags as there were up in the cliché, dusty attic, everything seemed to be labeled. Her husband, Steve—and Mike's stepdad for over twenty years—who had passed away ten years prior, must have placed most of this up here years ago.

The untouched boxes of childhood memorabilia, holiday décor, old magazines and other trinkets packed away was a sad sight. Sad, not because his mother was dead, but because Mike had no help with any of this. He couldn't afford a dumpster or to hire movers to take everything back to his studio apartment, which clearly lacked the room. He could hardly fit in the small space himself. But Mike started to feel guilty for thinking so.

The bulb hanging from the oars and brightness from one small window allowed him just enough light to fully see what he was looking at. Mike laughed to himself, thinking of his mother's militant yet tidy hoarding ways. He immediately went to the multiple boxes labeled "Mikey's stuff."

Years ago, she had mentioned the boxes to him, asking if he wanted any of it. He had told her no, repeatedly, but she apparently never got rid of them. Before ending every call, she would always ask how his writing was going.

"It's going great, Mom. I have a good feeling about this one." That had been his response every time. With every submission, every inquiry, he had known this was it. But it was *never* it.

He had landed a dead-end desk job, living the nine-to-five American dream and barely making ends meet. Though he continued to try, Mike never had the heart to tell her maybe he had made a mistake.

It had been different when he was a kid and would show her his poems and stories. Steve never seemed to give a shit, but at least pretended to be supportive when Mike's mom was around. Mike should have squashed the idea of becoming a writer long ago, but what happened during his childhood had made him continue.

He put his memories to a halt, and began to open one of the boxes. Mike was no longer a young man, but would always go back to that place in his mind where it turned into a dead end. He became sad his memories were already deteriorated, and grew even more depressed. His number one fan—his *only* fan—his mom, was gone.

Mike found some old, folded shirts. They must have been from when he was in grade school. Maybe a little older. He removed them from the top of the box's contents. Underneath were stacks of journals and composition notebooks.

"Holy shit!" His voice echoed in the attic, down the ladder to the rest of the house.

He had journaled from a young age, even remembered the notebooks, but Mike had never realized he had kept them. His *mother* keeping them, rather. He grabbed one from the top and flipped to a random page in the middle of the book:

Mom and Steve were total dicks today! I showed them a poem from the other day and Steve just rolled his eyes. Mom brought me aside and said to just show her from now on. Instead of helping Steve with his truck, like he always wanted, I just can't because I get so bored! I'll show them though. I keep trying to tell them I still can't sleep, but they don't want to listen. They don't want to hear what I have to say, ever. So, fuck them!!!

Mike chuckled to himself, flipping back a few pages. He hadn't written a poem in many decades, but he wondered which one had gained such disgust and disdain. His thumb found a page dated June 23, 1983:

The Gnawing stood tall
Wooden and brazen
Its face a clown with no make-up
Drooling for more
It takes the kids
Bagging up their teeth
Chasing me to an underworld
And then I wonder
Why does no one help me?

Mike closed the notebook abruptly. The Gnawing's eyes and mouth popped into his memory, rising up through the dirt of his trauma. His heart began to speed up, pounding in unison with an on-set headache. Mike felt sick but curious at the same time and grabbed the box, bringing it down from the attic.

Jesus, maybe I should read all of this shit from when I was twelve and then write a better manuscript for these blood-sucking publishers. Mike slammed the box down on the floor. He went to the fridge and cracked open a beer.

His nerves were unsettled, and he fought against remembering. At the same time, however, he wanted to recall, but only segments ran through his head. Mike continued to feel nauseous. Chugging the beer and rummaging through his mother's bar seemed like the perfect remedy.

I should probably just read more for inspiration, he thought.

Mike found a bottle of something stronger than beer and brought the container of life-saving liquid to the couch. He took a hearty swig and fingered through the many notebooks.

One entry was dated three years prior to the poem about the Gnawing Mike's disappointment regarding his parents.

February 5, 1980

When I first encountered the Gnawing, it was in a dream. Its towering legs looked like wood, connecting to just a smiling face with saliva dripping down from its teeth. The spit was shiny and reflective, burning my eyes to look at. It's like those drama masks I see at school. A permanent frown, then smile, blinking back and forth, changing and not making any sense, as I think a dream just does.

It wants their teeth

It wants their brain

But no one will ever know

Because they'll think I'm insane!

February 20, 1980

I saw it in the hallways at school today. It was just like it was in my dream. I left Ms. Benson's boring math class and it was eating the eyeballs from Matthew Harris's face. It picked away at Matthew's mouth, spitting out his teeth into one of those plastic sandwich bags, like the ones Mom packs for me. I tried to scream for help, but everyone just continued walking down the hall. The Gnawing saw me and raised its body, walking toward me faster and faster. As I turned around to run, I couldn't help but notice no one else noticed!

Everyone was heading to lunch or class or the bathroom, ignoring the fact that a monster was amongst us. My legs felt like cement. I kept looking around for someone to help me, to help Matthew. But as the monster came closer, I found a toilet to hide on.

I told Mom about it tonight and of course she didn't BELIEVE ME. She said I have to write down my stories, not tell them. IT ISN'T A STORY! I write this as I am about to go to sleep. If I don't wake up, I hope Mom and Steve read this first. They never believe me.

Mike closed the notebook and took a swig of brown liquor. The face of the Gnawing became much clearer in his mind, but he also appreciated it as just a story he had written at such a young age.

A *thunk* from above interrupted his thoughts. It was windy and Mike figured the noise was the old house. Perhaps the flooring expanding and then deflating from him opening the attic door for the first time in probably ten years.

Still nervous, still intrigued, Mike grabbed another random journal and opened it to yet another random page.

December 15, 1985

It found me walking home today
The silver snow
Robbed from swallowing me whole
But the Gnawing still there
Stomping and straining
Spitting up teeth like bullets
I tripped up stairs
Another nightmare that's life

I found a molar in my hair

Mike did the math. He must have been high school age at this point. There were years' worth of notebooks in this box, and though the memories came flooding back, it wasn't like what he had written about had *actually* happened. But the drunker he got, he knew what he did write about, he actually did see.

Jesus, no wonder Steve thought I was a psycho, he thought.

"Hey Mom! Ya shoulda put me on meds!" Mike yelled, to no one, except himself, and the pictures of family on his mother's mantle. His eyes locked in on the framed picture of his younger self, Steve and his mom. "You let me write, though! Too bad I fucked that up too!"

Mike stopped himself from throwing the precious bottle of booze. Deciding right then and there, he would drink himself to sleep and continue packing up his dead mother's house in the morning.

Thunk.

Another noise woke Mike from a snoring sleep. It was still dark outside, and the bottle was right where he had left it—on the floor next to the box of his childhood writings. His bladder throbbed.

Mike headed to the downstairs bathroom just off the hallway. He took a quick look by the door, realizing he had never put the stairs to the attic back up. The light had been left on, illuminating the stairway up to the second story of the house. It confirmed what he had already thought about the attic.

Fuck it.

After doing his business, Mike washed his face and stared at his reflection in the bathroom mirror. His pores thirsty from dehydration, matched his puffy eyes and the dark circles protruding from his face.

Mike pondered how he got here. He started thinking about the Gnawing again, remembered seeing the monster in his dreams as a young child, then on and off in his waking life into his teenage years.

Steve had died a little after Mike's first semester of college, and that was one of the first times the Gnawing had stopped appearing. Mike took two semesters off to stay home with his mother. Her devastation from Steve's death had left her almost catatonic for a month.

Finally graduating college later than planned, Mike eventually saved enough money for an apartment all to himself in the city, to pursue his writing career. He expected to work some shit job for a short amount of time. Flash forward over a decade later, Mike was still in the same shithole apartment, visiting his mother less and less since he had nothing to show of his writing success.

He flicked off the bathroom light. A dragging sound stopped him in his tracks, like chains heaving above him. It chilled him to the bone, and every hair on his body stood on end.

Nah!

Mike plopped back on the couch, staring at the journals and his mom's half-drank bottle of scotch. He was about to grab a notebook from the bottom of the box when he heard a noise again. The thud began to anger him, as opposed to scaring him like it did earlier. Mike ignored it and grabbed the notebook, opening it to the last few pages.

June 10, 1990

Steve seems much more sick today than he ever has. Mom keeps a positive attitude, though I hear her cry through the walls at night. My friends are all going to different colleges or staying in town like retards.

I got accepted to the institute of arts but a part of me just wants to lay down and stay in bed forever. In free period today, I went to the water fountain and I saw it again. I saw the Gnawing. It had been months.

As I pressed the button for water, I turned my head for just a second and it was there.

I blinked and blinked and blinked again. Each time I blinked, it spread its towering legs and got closer. It passed the closed doors of classrooms and thundered toward me as everyone else in study hall just studied away. My hand was still pressing the fountain and water continued to spurt while I looked back at the ACTUAL people going about their day.

As the Gnawing ducked under an exit sign, it got so close to me I could smell its breath. I do believe this was the first time it was this close to me. I was officially frozen in fear, more than I had ever been since I was eight years old. I thought it was over. I thought it was just a nightmare, as these images of the monster disappeared with age. But there it was. Right in front of me.

I was about to scream out, not caring about the social life I already lacked. It took a hold of my face with its gnashing teeth and threw me to the ground.

Mike put his hand to his face and traced the faint scars with his fingertips.

That's right. Everyone thought I tripped and smashed my face on the floor. Mom was so upset. Upset that I was hurt, but also because my graduation pictures looked like a nightmare all on their own.

Closing yet another journal abruptly, Mike tried to remember what the Gnawing had whispered to him before taking a chunk out of his face.

What was it? What the hell was it? And why didn't I write it down?

His thoughts were panicky. Mike started picking up each notebook and throwing them about, realizing that was the last entry. He could go back and catalog all his early years until the last few days of high school, but at this point, it would still just cause more questions with very little answers from his younger self.

Another scratching and dragging sound from above could not be ignored at this point.

Mike grabbed the bottle of scotch and got up from the sofa. Before moving toward the stairs, he looked at the framed portrait of his mother on the mantle. She was young in the picture and looked genuinely happy. The scratching sounds seemed fainter now, and Mike figured moving all the boxes around must have unleashed a family of mice.

Determined to stop his thoughts, the mice, and everything else, he marched up to the second floor and started toward the attic.

The light was still on from earlier. Mike bent down to avoid the oars, gripping his bottle of booze to his chest like a shield. Still buzzed, he squinted and scanned the attic. His vision was not exactly blurry, but it also wasn't clear. Mike went over to the pile of boxes marked with his name and vigorously moved them around to find the mouse.

Nothing.

When he stood up from his knees, Mike heard a much louder scratching sound. Like something dragging against the floor and echoing within the scarcely insulated walls.

Mike turned around and focused on the other piles of boxes, knowing it would be difficult to locate a mouse. Buying traps would be added to his to-do list for tomorrow.

"You will know it. When you see me. You will know it. When you see me."

Mike's heart stopped when he heard the whispers. He couldn't decide if it actually happened or if his broken memories and drunkenness in the seemingly haunted house were just getting to him.

"You will know it when you see me. *You will know it when you see me!*" The whispers became more intense-sounding, and Mike dropped the bottle of scotch.

He cupped his hands to his ears and watched the bottle roll toward some boxes in the corner of the attic. With his eyes closed his eyes tight, Mike sank down with his elbows to his knees, like a scared child.

Then there was silence.

Mike opened his eyes slowly, expecting to see a ghost, a mouse, or perhaps even the Gnawing. But once he was able to focus, he only saw boxes marked "***STEVE***" in messy black lettering.

He pushed up from his knees, and stood, then slowly walked over to Steve's boxes. The bottle of scotch was miraculously unbroken. Mike popped it open, took another girthy sip, and opened a box on top of the pile.

A few photo albums, crocheted napkins, and other bubble-wrapped random knick-knacks...even some old sports cards possibly worthy of selling...

Mike's sudden bout of rage mixed with confusion. Furious, he kicked the box away, then went through the second "Steve" box and a third.

"It's all the same shit, isn't it? Isn't it!" Mike's emotions hit an all-time high, and he chugged yet another swig of the scotch. He stared at the last cardboard box marked "Steve."

The grief, anger, confusion, and sadness combined with fear of what he had been experiencing in the last day—along with childhood monsters—made for a poorly mixed cocktail of a man. In the attic of his dead mother's house, no less.

Fuck it, he thought.

Mike slowly picked apart the cardboard flaps and reached inside for the contents. A neatly folded flannel blanket covered in sawdust sat on top.

Weird, but okay, Stepdad Steve!

Mike's thoughts raced, and he hoped to stop feeling guilty for his reactions. Resentment and regret were always inevitable from birth up until death. But when Mike pulled out the third flannel blanket, something small fell out and clanked on the floor.

"What the hell?"

Mike looked to his left, then to his right, and saw it, sparkling from the dim attic light. His eyes widened, and his chest became tight.

It was a tooth.

He removed the fourth blanket from the box, uncovering six zippered plastic baggies filled with teeth. All different shapes and sizes—molars, pre-molars, canines. Some pearly white, some tarnished yellow, some even filled with silver or gold. Some discolored with a stained, coagulated brown. Mike took out each plastic bag from the box, determined to get to the bottom of this cardboard hellhole. He placed each bag of teeth on the ground, realizing this was the final reveal.

"You will know it."

Mike ignored the whispers making a comeback.

"When you see me!"

Mike lifted the final bag and saw it. He saw the Gnawing.

Its wooden legs had been folded like a doll at the bottom of Steve's box, with its head and face crooked and turned down. Frozen with fear, Mike knew even if he picked it up and stretched it out, the figure in the box could only measure to about three feet tall. The Gnawing he remembered had been at least ten feet. This coming from the perspective of his high-school-aged self who had been much more logical than his younger version.

Mike stared at the remnants, attempting to wrap his mind around what he had literally just un-boxed. His heart pounded faster and faster, and he looked back and forth from the bags of teeth to the puppet-looking, laughable Gnawing replica.

A clattering, heaving noise, though faint, started to sneak up behind Mike.

He figured it was the notorious mouse, and once again ignored the attic sounds that had been bothering him all night. Mike continued to stare at Steve's hidden contents.

The Gnawing's wooden leg slid up the ladder leading to the attic. Its second leg followed, stretching like a snake. It bowed beneath the eaves, and its perpetual smile gawked at Mike's back. It pictured the fear and confusion within the human's kneeling body amongst the boxes, grit, and treasure bags that had been packed away for decades.

The block-like feet bolstered the towering, bent legs of the Gnawing. It slowly leaned down, inches away from the back of Mike's neck. The creature's breath created goosepimples on Mike's skin.

"When you see me..."

Mike immediately turned around, making eye contact with the true monster.

It smelled his face, the scars with a familiar scent, the creature receded and stood as tall as it could inside the attic.

Slow tears streamed down Mike's face just before the Gnawing lunged toward him.

"...you will know."

Survivor

The 32nd Floor

Ted Simmons locked the door behind him, then ran to meet his two partners at the elevators. Shutting the power off for just the one floor had been easier than he thought it would be. Getting the fuck out of Dodge before anyone noticed anything had happened was going to be the hard part. His heart pounded as his two "friends" dressed in the same maintenance garb, covered the rolling trash bin with the contents they had "obtained."

Kevin, the tallest of the three men, checked his watch. "Thirty floors to the van and we can get the hell out of here. We have about five minutes 'til this place is lit back up."

Ted nodded in acknowledgment, then looked at Darren. He and Kevin both seemed so cool, calm, and collected. Ted tried to give off that impression, but the sweat pouring down his face was a dead giveaway.

"Hey Teddy-boy, don't *worry*. Boss'll be happy. Kev here will be happy, which means: *we'll all be happy*." Darren had an annoying arrogance about him. His voice always got high-pitched in certain syllables when he was trying to convince others of something.

"Don't call me Kev. And I'll be happy once we're driving away in the van, with this piece-of-shit city in the rearview." Kevin pressed the down button a few more times. His impatience grew; so did the red in his face.

Ted wasn't typically intimidated by many people. Kevin, on the other hand, was a whole other animal. Literally. Ted had watched him beat the teeth out of two security guards at their last job. It was a shift change—a mistake that would *not* happen again. Ted would never forget pointing out to Kevin he had part of a canine lodged in one of his knuckles on the drive home.

He had known Kevin could snap at any moment, and the nonchalance displayed with the teeth and the blood, it was only a matter of time until Kevin would once again reveal his true self. Kevin was militant in every aspect of his life and all the jobs the trio had worked on together. But if there was one surprise, one overlooked plan, people just happened to get beaten to death. Ted had thought this was a liability, but the violence always ended up saving their asses.

"*Woohoo*! We're almost home-free, motherfuckers!" Darren yelled, jumping up and down, interrupting Ted's thoughts.

Kevin shot his look to Darren, which of course shut him up immediately.

The elevator doors opened, and Ted's heart sank when there was a woman standing inside. The building should have been empty at this point.

Now fucking what? He walked in first, smiling at the woman who gripped her purse and looked up to see what floor they were on. Ted quickly turned to Kevin and Darren, who adjusted their work shirts to cover the firearms they had tucked away.

The 53rd Floor

Jane McCoy stared at the debriefing on her computer, then finally noticed the time. She hit send, grabbed her purse, and flew out of the office, knowing Stan and the kids would once again be pissed at another late night in the office. Though the whole point of her taking the promotion had been for more food on the table, more vacations, and all in all, a better future for herself and the family, the guilt of being away from them weighed on her like a thick tar.

Ignoring her feelings, she thumbed the down button outside the elevator, tapping her foot to relieve herself from the anxiety of her family's disappointment and what the other partners in the firm would think of the research she sent to them in the debriefing. The *ting-ting* of the elevator case moving its way to her snapped Jane out of her thoughts, calming her, letting her know she was just a few steps away from being back home.

The doors opened, and Jane stepped into the cart, adjusting the purse strap to her shoulder. Jane muttered, "Fuck!" when the elevator doors closed, once she realized how truly late in the night it was.

Fifty floors and counting. The parking garage containing her beautiful luxury car, that *she* had earned was just minutes away. Jane fumbled through her purse, wanting to contact her husband and let him know she was *really* on her way home this time. The elevator cart shaking a bit, the lights flickering for a second, didn't alarm Jane. She swore, as modern as the entire office building was, management should have hired different engineers for the damn elevators.

Thirty-five...thirty-four...thirty-three...The elevator shook a little more, then the familiar *ting!* It had stopped at the thirty-second floor.

It's after midnight. Who in the hell is still here? Jane thought, realizing her phone was not in her purse. She was also confused. Half the floors of the building typically remained empty after five—bank offices—employees from the other companies continued to work from home.

The elevator doors opened, revealing three men of fairly large stature, all dressed in black.

Great, Jane thought. *This is all I need.*

One of the men nodded at Jane then looked at the others with widening eyes. The two reciprocated the surprise but tried to act normal, pushing their cleaning cart through the elevator doors.

Jane edged back to the farthest corner of the elevator cart, gripping her purse like a weapon, keeping her best I'm-not-afraid-of-anything look on her face. She stared at the numbered buttons, not making eye contact with the men. Jane calculated how many more floors she had to go, and her pulse started to rise.

In the attempt to calm herself, she thought, *It's just a cleaning crew, and there's nothing to worry about! Don't be a dummy.*

She studied the backs of their necks, but when she looked up at the tallest man, her palms began to sweat.

Should I just press the button for the next floor? Or just fucking wait until I get to my car?

It's always that fine line between paranoia and instinct which tends to blur while your body catches up during the decision-making process. Jane's survival instincts were frozen because instead of concentrating on the keys in her purse, she just locked in on the screen above the elevator doors, which was counting down to the parking garage.

The elevator continued to descend. The shortest of the three men kept looking at Jane, then back at the tallest man.

"Hey, Ted! You hear about the Kings? They're totally *tanking* out east right now!" The shorter man said, slapping the man of mid-height.

"Yeah. Well—"

The elevator slowed, shuddering with a deafening, metal scraping. Then, everything went black.

Jane silently gasped while one of the men yelled, "Shit!"

There was an electric smell, and the lights flickered on, the elevator coming to an abrupt stop.

Jane quickly moved toward the panel to press the emergency button, when Kevin immediately pushed the cleaning cart out of his way and grabbed her by the throat.

"We're not going to be doing that today." Kevin's pupils enlarged, staring into Jane's small, blue eyes.

She wanted to cry but somehow kept her composure when his grip tightened around her neck.

"*Yo*. Not right now," Ted said trying to intervene. "Something must have happened with the power. We're still twenty floors away. Let's not fuck this up again." Ted grabbed Kevin's shoulder and he released Jane.

Darren moved the cleaning cart to the furthest side and tried pressing the button that was supposed to lead to the bottom floor and parking garage. Nothing happened. "Do we try the doors?"

"*No*. You're literally *not* supposed to fucking do that." Ted was sure too. He didn't feel like babysitting a woman, Darren's antics, and whatever plans Kevin had.

Kevin looked down at his watch. "Less than three minutes and no contingency. This is on you, Theodore. What's the next move?"

Ted looked at Jane, his heart rate picking up pace. They could either open the elevator hatch and abandon what they had come here for, or they could wait for help and kill everyone in the way. *Or* they could figure out what was wrong with the elevator and make it down the twenty floors, all while keeping Kevin away from their unexpected guest.

Jane coughed, while rubbing her throat, gluing herself to the walls of the elevator cart. There was no escape, and all hope was leaving her mind. Any scenario matching her fate was not a promising one. Jane figured she'd just keep her mouth shut, and if one of them decided to go after her again, she'd do her best and die trying.

She almost wanted to laugh, watching the three grown men argue about what to do next. When they stopped paying attention to her, she was about to reach her arm and jump toward the emergency call button, but then the elevator cart made a horrible screeching sound and slowly began to descend. Again.

The elevator shook violently, and the cleaning cart the men had brought in rolled toward Jane. All three men swayed out of it way and tried to grab the cart. The elevator began descending abnormally fast.

The lights started to flicker, and the elevator cart gained momentum. Jane just crouched, bringing her knees to chest, and silently cried. *I'm going to die with these idiots*, she thought.

All four occupants gasped when the walls shook, making it feel like airplane turbulence. The overspeed brakes locked up, which pulled the men's cleaning cart back to the furthest corner from Jane, knocking Darren to the floor. His head whipped back against the wall, and before he could put his hands out in defense, the bottom corner of the cleaning cart pierced his face. It was a clean stab, like a chef's knife going through a slushy. The force of it all sprayed blood on the other three people.

Ted regained his balance as the elevator cart slowed down. Floor "10" it read. They weren't too far up at this point. "Kevin, press the fucking emergency button We'll figure the rest out!

Jane wiped the blood from her face, stopping herself from panicking. She stood up and watched the shorter man spewing blood from his face like a hose spicket. The tall man, ignoring the demands from the other, maneuvered the cleaning cart so he was next to the dead one. The cart in between Ted and Jane blocked them from being able to press the call button for help.

"We're opening the door before we crash to the ground. Whatever safeties this fuckin thing has, I'll kill you both before our plan is ruined." Kevin yelled, gripping the cleaning cart tighter. He shifted his eyes back and forth between Jane and Ted.

Darren's body finally stopped twitching and plopped sideways to the floor. The crack of his shoulder slamming against the ground startled everyone. Jane and Ted watched Kevin. The floor reader that had stuck on "10" moved to "9" in a startling, eerie silence.

Though they were only around nine or ten floors up, the cable already snapped, the brakes of the elevator held steady. Below it—and them all—was a safe air pocket. Then, and only then, could they pry the doors open, which would usher them into the parking garage they were readily awaiting.

Though the brakes were holding steady, the elevator cart began to slowly shake again.

"Kevin. Hold our shit all you want, but we need to get out of here alive to get paid. Darren's already dead. We can make it out of here only a few stories up. Let's hit that red button and jump out the damn shaft."

"No. This bitch is a liability. Boss won't like it. You take care of her and I'll stack the boost."

Jane, unaware of what the men were speaking of, quickly grabbed the keys from her purse and pointed the tiny knife keychain toward them both. "I don't give a shit what you all are doing. But I'm pretty sure we're all gonna die at this point if we follow your *instructions...*"

The elevator cart rumbled another time. Kevin pushed the cleaning cart in Ted's direction and headed toward Jane in a few fast, wobbling steps. He grabbed her by the hips, pulled her toward him, then threw her upward. She dropped to the ground hard—and unconscious.

The elevator fell to the last few stories, the inside lights blinking their ghostly glare. Ted grabbed the cleaning cart while Kevin tried to balance himself, grabbing for the pistol sitting snug in the back of his pants.

With his hand reaching behind him, the cleaning cart lunged forward and pinned him against the edge of the floor buttons, where the elevator doors met the corners. Ted heard the crack of Kevin's elbow and leaped toward him just as the elevator hit the air pocket right above the concrete parking garage floor.

Jane awoke, feeling woozy, but kept her eyes closed and hoped for the best. Or at least, for a quick death.

The elevator cart bounced, throwing all four bodies in opposite directions. Jane rolled to the left; Ted was thrown over the cleaning cart. Kevin had just jerked his pistol out, pulling the trigger in mid-air, hitting Ted square in the forehead. When the bullet hit Ted, the cleaning cart lifted a couple of feet, piercing Kevin through his larynx.

While Jane lay against the cold wall, the elevator doors opened a few inches. Then closed. Continuously opening and closing, like some sick, mechanical joke. She felt like a mangled pretzel, attempting to gather her thoughts, staring before her at a carnage of bloodied, distorted bodies.

Jane propped herself up to stand, wobbled over, and leaned to push the emergency button. *You know, the one that should have been pressed thirty floors up!* She thought to herself, then laughed out loud.

She kept laughing, ignoring the pain in her mouth and ribs, but stopped herself from pressing the button. Jane removed the canvas from atop the cleaning cart. It appeared to be covering dozens of computer hard drives, USB flash drives, and other various parts—some labeled "*Property of Lockley Bank: If Found, Call: 1-800-523-5523.*"

The elevator doors would not stop opening and closing, but they did not expand wide or slowly enough for her to escape. Jane hit the emergency call button, her finger shaking. Seconds felt like years until a technician was finally on the other end of the speaker,

"Hello? Are you okay in there? There seemed to have been an odd power outage in the entire building."

"Yes! *Yes! I'm here,*" Jane shrieked. "They're dead! They're all dead! Please fucking help me!"

"It's okay, ma'am. Emergency services are on their way. You're not dead."

"I know *I'm* not dead! *They are!*"

"They?"

Jane was about to speak again but the static sound of the call ending, interrupted her. She looked at the elevator doors, then shimmied the cleaning cart out of the way, trying to pivot it in the right position to keep the doors open.

Sirens echoed throughout the parking garage, and that glimmer of hope sparked within the sweat coming out of her palms. *Please, just get me out of here.* The cleaning cart was too big, too awkward to keep the doors open. Jane just waited, pressing the emergency call button over and over staring at the dead men in front of her.

Radio silence. And surrounded by the dead.

The sirens became louder and louder, and Jane began to just yell. The clanking of the elevator doors, the silent pools of blood becoming bigger and bigger...She thought she was losing her mind. Her head pounding and body sore from the night's events, Jane tried to keep screaming for help, but her throat closed up due to the lack of moisture.

When the sirens no longer sang their tune, Jane stood and listened for her rescue. She thought she heard footsteps and the sounds of vehicles swerving down to where the elevator had crash-landed. The doors stopping and a voice on the emergency speaker broke her thoughts.

"*Ma'am*! Are you still there? The senior technician is on his way along with paramedics."

"I'm...I'm here. Please hurry."

"Should be less than two minutes. Hang tight!"

Ground Floor

Joe Keene along with his partner and driver, Delia Vasquez, got the radio about the fire department being stuck in the middle of an accident off Madison.

"Of course, they're stuck. They wouldn't know how to drive if the truck was the size of one of those smart cars."

Joe laughed at Delia's remark, knowing full well she could back it up. That's why she drove the rig and he was their guide for everything else.

Delia parked while Joe tried radioing the technician. The elevator emergency dispatch had said the on-call guy wasn't too far away and would meet them there. As always, Joe and Delia had no idea what they were walking into. *It's part of the job*, Joe always told himself.

"Hey, that must be him."

Delia looked up from unfolding the stretcher to confirm what Joe had said. A man in utility gear, carrying a tool-box waved from a distance, then pointed to his left where the elevator shaft was. Both could hear the clanking of doors from where they stood.

Joe felt a pit in his stomach the closer they got to the technician. He wasn't sure if it was the bad coffee he had earlier or just the feeling of impending doom he experienced each time before stepping into a scene.

"Hey, man. F.D. is stuck out there. I think P.D. should be here soon. But I guess you can get this fixed before the amateurs show up! Do we know what we're looking at?" Joe always impressed himself, the way he faked his confident tone.

"I'm not sure. I know there's at least one person stuck inside. Some kind of power outage knocked it off its kilter," the technician stated.

"All right, good sir! You lead the way! Vasqez, you got that?"

"Yeah, yeah. I'm following you. As always." Delia pushed the stretcher, walking alongside Joe.

The two followed the technician, and about ten or so feet away from the elevator, a loud *bang* echoed around them.

Joe suddenly fell to the pavement, face-first. Delia stopped in her tracks, her brain slowly processing what had just happened. She turned to the technician who was pointing the gun at her.

A second *bang*. Delia also killed in an instant.

The technician put his cell phone to his ear. "Contingency in place. Grabbing the boost now. Problem will be solved in less than five minutes. Call you in twenty."

The Elevator

Jane had positioned herself in the farthest corner of the elevator cart, making sure to be as far away from the bodies as humanly possible. She sat, clutching her ankles. Her face was buried in her knees, but she abruptly rose when as she heard muffled voices and what sounded like two shots.

Gun shots?

That missing survival instinct finally flared to life, and though her chest tightened, nausea kicking in, she sprang up and grabbed the pistol the tall man had dropped right before he met his demise.

"Hello? Is anyone there? I'm about to fix the doors and get you out!" The voice sounded calm and stern.

Hesitating, Jane slowly moved to another corner.

"I...I'm here. I don't know what happened...People are dead. *They're dead*!"

"It's okay, ma'am," the technician continued. "We'll get you out of there in no time." He placed his tool-box on the ground, and grabbed both a flange and a door wedge. After he propped the tools in place, the doors finally stopped moving. The elevator cart itself was wedged up a bit, but he was able to just about walk through and place his hand out to Jane. "Ma'am? We don't have much time. Take my hand. Fire and EMT are here," he lied.

Jane emerged from the shadows, her left hand hiding behind her back, while she reached forward with her right. The technician pulled her with such force, her shoulder came out of socket. The pain shot through her entire body, making her forget he threw her down to the concrete. Literally seeing stars, Jane lay there unmoving, unable to comprehend or contemplate a next move—unsure if she even had a chance for a next move.

With the doors now open, the technician jumped into the elevator cart, hauled the cleaning bin out, and pushed it a few feet away from himself and Jane. He had about a minute to finish her, load the boost into his van and leave successfully.

The technician crouched on top of her and flopped Jane's body over so she was facing him. This was one of his favorite—and least favorite—parts of his job. Tears pooled from her closed eyelids, he steadied his aim, standing and about to shoot, but his ears suddenly began to ring.

Gunsmoke filled his nostrils, burning his eyes. The technician's world went black and he dropped to his knees.

Jane watched the man's eyes roll back into his head. Her left arm trembled, holding the gun, ready to fire again. When the wet plop made its distinct sound, Jane screamed. The kill was confirmed. Confused, all she could do was lie there in pain.

A couple of minutes went by, but there were still no police. No official help, at least not yet.

Jane balanced herself back up to her feet, quivering. She spat at the elevator, kicked the cleaning bin, and turned around. Realizing the morbidity of dead lying behind her, in front of her, she dropped the gun.

And continued to wait.

Side Effects

Kyla Jackson stared at her phone in disbelief. She scrolled through the screen-shots sent to her containing messages from her wife's apparent lover, and her face grew red and hot. Kyla's heart pounded faster and faster. She stood outside the hospital waiting room standing by for her wife to be wheeled out of surgery.

Kyla had had her suspicions on and off for the last year or so but had chalked it up to paranoia. She knew Rochelle excelled at gaslighting, but she was also apparently adept at faking how much they needed each other. The woman who sent the messages hadn't said much, but didn't have to. It looked like she was fed up with Rochelle too.

This was what social media is good for, right? There was never a good time for it, but as Kyla figured she could quickly go through her wife's phone to confirm the new and shocking information. The laptop was only a short drive away.

But then Kyla got the ping on her own phone. The surgery was over. And successful.

The wheels of the hospital bed squeaked on the newly sanitized floor into the recovery room. Rochelle Petersen struggled to keep her eyes open, the anesthesia slowly starting to leave her system. Drugged and groggy, she attempted to answer the nurse when asked what level of pain she was in. The surgery had taken a little longer than expected, and Rochelle hurt more than she'd figured she would. She opened her eyes slowly, and the nurse fed the IV painkillers, then offered her some ice chips.

Rochelle gathered her thoughts. She couldn't wait to see Kyla and receive the reassurance from her. Rochelle could always count on Kyla for that. The need for comfort from her—and whoever else—started to make Rochelle nauseous. Or maybe it was the painkillers kicking in. Rochelle closed her eyes again, and drifted off in a half sleep, relaxed and tense all at the same time.

"Rochelle. Rochelle! Take some deep breaths again. What level is your pain now?"

The nurse, still by her side sounded compassionate but also annoyed Rochelle. If she hadn't felt so nauseous, Rochelle would have laughed at herself for still feeling irritable, even after just having major surgery.

Rochelle was eventually wheeled into another room, a little more aware and awake. The next nurse was less irritating and kept the small talk limited, but stayed attentive. Another half an hour went by and Kyla wasn't there. Rochelle began to panic inside and let anxiety take over.

Where is she? Did something happen? I don't have anyone to help take care of me. I can't even walk, for Christ's sake. Rochelle questioned the protocol of the hospital and let the panic continue to seep into her thoughts like a tsunami.

Kyla walked in the room. Her mouth was smiling, and her eyes looked concerned. "Hi, baby!"

Rochelle let out a sigh of relief and returned a grin. She couldn't say much. The pain meds were coursing through her body, and she felt dizzy. Rochelle reached out her hand, and Kyla gently squeezed back while listening to the discharge instructions from the nurse.

———————

Kyla gripped the steering wheel so tight the entire drive home, her forearms ached. Her thoughts continued to race. It took every ounce of energy she had to fake being okay and not show a single shed of emotion other than happiness and relief the surgery had gone well. The only saving grace were the drugs still in Rochelle's system. The grogginess would last for at least a couple of days.

But Kyla knew how stubborn and observant her wife was. Fooling her for now would be tough, but Kyla didn't have a plan yet either. Rochelle was physically powerless and dependent on Kyla for rest and recovery. At least, that's what she figured. Who knew if Rochelle had any back-up bitches on speed dial.

After multiple "Thank yous" and "I love yous," Kyla was able to get Rochelle into bed comfortably. Rochelle had always been an outwardly affectionate person, and in her weakened state, this became multiplied. If Rochelle hadn't been cheating on her, Kyla would have reciprocated the tenderness. She had already been prepared to be at her wife's beck and call, but now, all she could do was fantasize about smothering Rochelle with a pillow.

The hurt and rage burned inside her chest. Kyla wanted to scream and break shit. But she didn't. She appeared calm on the outside. Once Rochelle's snoring started, she would do some detective work and figure out the next move.

Kyla had made sure to put Rochelle's phone on the nightstand right next to her wife. She didn't want to start this disgusting infiltration by going through the phone and raising suspicion.

Once she had confirmation of Rochelle being dead asleep, Kyla was able to sob in silence. She signed into her wife's messages via their laptop.

It's true. Kyla thought. *You lying, nasty cunt.*

Tears waterfalled down her checks. She read message after message, saw picture after picture. Tears soaked the front of her shirt, like a pool of wet shame and depression. Kyla had her confirmation and slammed the laptop closed. She double-checked Rochelle's snoring and quickly left the house to get the prescriptions for her two-timing, whore wife.

———————

After coming back from the pharmacy, Kyla sat in her car, staring at their house illuminated by the car's headlights. It was winter now and the light snow began to fall. Kyla became entranced by the snowflakes dancing in the wind, and her heartrate finally returned to a normal beat. She knew she would have to take care of her wife of ten plus years, then leave her. But she also knew she wouldn't be able to control her actions due to her emotions, which admittedly, had been a problem for both of them.

Kyla contemplated her next move between sadness and feeling vengeful. The snow was falling heavy now. It felt like only minutes had passed, but when she saw the ground covered in white, she went to grab the bag of medications and head inside. Kyla had three missed calls on her phone.

"Fuck!"

Kyla's plotting—or the lack thereof—had gotten away from her, and what seemed like minutes, had actually been two hours. She ran inside, clutching her phone, purse, and Rochelle's prescriptions.

"Babe! Babe! I'm so sorry! Are you okay?"

"Hey."

"There was a fucking accident on Route 9, and my goddamn phone was on silent. Plus, there's a blizzard happening..." Kyla was surprised how easily the lies just spilled from her tongue. Proud of herself, she thought, *I learn from the best.*

"I just needed to pee...but didn't make it." Rochelle's words slurred slightly, but she mustered enough strength to point to her lower body and the damp spot on the bed sheets.

"Fuck, woman. I am so sorry. Let's get this cleaned up. I got you your meds, and they gave you the good stuff at least."

"Okayyyy."

Rochelle seemed childlike in her response and didn't even sound mad. Kyla was thankful for modern medicine, as all of it kept her wife docile—something that was a rare trait with Rochelle.

"Okay, Petersen. Turn over one more time."

"When did you change my clothes?" Rochelle asked, genuinely confused.

"Don't worry about it. You're cleaned up and the bed is fresh. Here, take this." Kyla handed her wife a pain pill and a plastic tumbler of ice water.

Two days passed. Though Kyla cried herself to sleep at night on the couch on the other side of the house, she was able to encase her rage when in the presence of her wife. She dutifully assisted Rochelle to the bathroom, helped bathe and dress her, and did whatever Rochelle needed while she was pumped full of medication and barely mobile.

What Rochelle didn't know, was Kyla slowly doubling the dose of medications—enough to keep Rochelle euphoric and docile, but also enough to keep her conscious and able to have conversations.

Kyla waited until the seventh day after her wife's surgery to let her plan fall into place. She lay in bed with Rochelle, going over the list she was writing for the store. Kyla surprised herself by not letting on to her knowledge of her wife's affairs and indiscretions. She was also impressed she could "fake" a grocery list.

"All right, so we have plenty of coffee. Do you want more juice or ginger ale?" Kyla even batted her eyes when she asked the question.

"Um, both, yeah, if you don't mind."

"All right, babe. I just have to get an oil change then I'll tackle this list. You sure you'll be okay?"

"I think so. I'm tired anyway, so I'll probably read, then nap. Thank you so much for everything. I'm starting to feel stronger already."

Rochelle stated this with such an oblivious confidence, but Kyla knew it was bullshit. The bitch couldn't even piss by herself yet.

"All right. My ringer is on. So just text or call if you think of anything else!"

"I will. Love you."

"Love you too."

Kyla dimmed the bedroom lights and closed the door. She had already crushed an extra pill in her wife's ginger ale to keep Rochelle passed out for longer than she should have been. *Let her lay there and soak in her own filth for a few hours. Then maybe she'll regret fucking someone else.* Kyla smirked to herself, adjusted the rearview mirror and backed out of the driveway.

After getting her car serviced, Kyla went to the mall. She browsed and window-shopped for an hour or so while continually checking her phone. Assuming Rochelle was asleep, she tried on a few outfits, then decided to treat herself to a beer and a burger.

Kyla felt so free. She could hardly remember what it had been like to be single. It had always been depressing. But now? Now she had a small taste of what it was like to not be tied down. Until the memories of those text messages and screenshots reared their ugly heads into her psyche...

She ordered another beer and finished her fries, deciding she'd wait until her bitch-wife contacted her. *The groceries can wait too.*

Rochelle woke from her nap and reached for her phone to check the time. She wasn't sure what time Kyla had left to run errands, but there was a throbbing pain in her abdomen.

Fuck.

Assuming it was her bladder again and nothing serious, Rochelle adjusted her body and reached for the remote, lifting the mattress into an upright position. Though she still felt the buzz of the medication, she also had the need to urinate. She yelled for Kyla but the house was silent. And then, it happened again.

Rochelle looked down at her legs. The warmth of urine created a slight puddle beneath her. She started to cry. Not only did she feel helpless, but she wondered why the hell her wife wasn't there. *Again.* This wasn't like Kyla, and though Rochelle consistently took her for granted, she wondered how she had even ended up like this. It wasn't like Kyla to not be by her side when she needed her. So Rochelle lay there, marinating in her own piss and, feeling sorry for herself.

Rochelle's thighs stuck together like glue, thanks to the urine. Her legs began to fuse together and weigh her down, but she was able to press the button on the remote to lower the bedframe. She lay flat, deciding whether she should try and make it to the bathroom by herself or bother her wife with another one of her mishaps. Rochelle tried to roll over on her side, but her lower body felt like cement.

"What the fuck is happening?" Rochelle continued to yell at herself, then pressed the button for the bedframe to lift back up, so at least her upper body would be more comfortable and she could see what was going on from a better angle.

The bed remote suddenly stopped working.

"Fucking batteries! Fucking bladder!" Rochelle cried more, then went to reach for her phone to call Kyla. It was across the room on the TV stand. As her legs continued to fuse together and become gray, all Rochelle could do was pass back out into a drug-induced coma.

A few hours later, Kyla was still not back home. Rochelle awoke with heavy eyelids, and as she blinked, she went to wipe away the crust from her eyes. But her arms weren't working. Panic began to set in and she yelled out for her wife yet again.

The silence was disturbing, the air was cold, and all Rochelle could hear was the wind beating the sides of their house. She felt a slimy membrane encase her lower body that crept into her wrists and forearms.

Did I piss myself again? She thought to herself as she tried to reason with reality.

She lifted her head to look down at herself. Her hands had bonded to her hips, covered in a milky mucus. The sludge oozed to her legs and feet, which looked like a sodden sarcophagus, not a pair of legs. Still able to move her upper back and shoulders, Rochelle banged that part of her body up and down out of frustration, with tears pouring over her cheeks.

She attempted to raise her lower body, but it was glued to the mattress by the thick substance, which only slightly lifted and sprung back down. It clung to Rochelle's skin like tar, and the pain forced her to stop the escape efforts. After seeing what she could and feeling what was happening, Rochelle wanted to risk trying to move again, possibly ripping the skin from her body but maybe allowing her to get to her phone.

This plan was quickly squashed when Rochelle finally realized how long it had actually been since Kyla had been home, as well as the last time she had had her medication. It had been at least half a day. Kyla always liked getting errands over with in the morning so she could relax and then make sure to be there in between Rochelle's naps.

Rochelle's muscles constricted and tightened, and more mucus secreted from her body. The pain surging through her became stronger, and everything shifted further, into a nightmare she couldn't seem to wake up from.

———————

Kyla pushed the shopping cart toward her car with a smirk. She had completed the list but made modifications. Everything she had purchased was mostly for her to bring back to the hotel room she had booked for herself, along with items her wife could use and eat on her own. *I'm not going to just abandon her. What am I, a monster?* Kyla packed up her car and pictured her plan for the next hour going down perfectly.

It began snowing again. The wet, fluffy flakes fell fast and hard, sprinkling the path home for Kyla. She adjusted her headlights and fog lights. All she could think about was the look that would be on Rochelle's face when Kyla showed her the messages on her phone and then her back when she left her. Rochelle had family who could come and take over, or one of the bitches she had fucked can feel free to help her to the toilet.

This is divorce, baby! Enjoy! And get well, bitch!

The road became slushy and wet. Kyla's SUV slid and wobbled a bit, but she pulled into the driveway and found herself staring at the house and the snow falling again.

Kyla's chest became tight, and tears filled her eyes. She pounded the steering wheel with the sides of her fists and screamed. Memories of the life they had built flooded her brain, and all she could do was continue to yell and cry. She hated herself for having left Rochelle alone for so long, but at the same time, Kyla couldn't decipher if her heart had just truly broken. She was unable to conceive ever having rational thought at this point.

The guilt and anger boiled inside of her, and just when she thought she was going to vomit, she remembered the greasy burger she had earlier. Any energy she had, was wasted on faking being okay in front of her wife, along with *taking care* of Rochelle post-surgery. The late nights had only allowed her to cry herself to sleep, just to get up in the morning to do it all over again.

Kyla wiped away her tears, along with the snot pouring down her chin, allowing herself to take deep breaths until her chest felt less tight. This is what she had to do. If there was one thing she did know, it was she would never be able to forgive or trust again. And this small act of revenge had tasted sweeter than anything else she had ever experienced. Kyla gained her composure, grabbed the few bags meant for Rochelle and trekked the few steps to the front door.

When she unlocked the door and walked in, she felt the eerie silence around her. The front porch light illuminated the snow falling, and their shadows danced through the living room window.

"Hey *babe*! I'm home, *babe*!"

Kyla dragged the grocery bags against the carpet floor dramatically to make sure Rochelle could hear her. She paused in her tracks. Her wife's whimpering echoed from the bedroom.

"Oh *babe*! I got everything you needed! *Babe*!"

Kyla, proud of her condescending and sarcastic tone, cracked open the bedroom door. The light from the hallway just barely shined on Rochelle's face—eyes bloodshot and tears streaming down her cheeks.

Kyla threw the groceries toward the side of the bed, and they bounced off the wall within perfect arm's length for Rochelle. Then, she reached in her pocket, grabbing her phone.

"Well. *Babe*. I talked with your buddy. More like, she talked with me." Kyla held up her phone from a few feet away, showing screenshot after screenshot of Rochelle's many discrepancies. "Some of these are almost a year old! But my favorite one is how you're telling this bitch a week before your surgery that when you 'get better'—*hah*... 'get better'—is that you can't wait to see her again!"

Rochelle just looked at Kyla with watery, blank eyes. She mumbled something, but Kyla couldn't quite make it out.

"I'm sorry, what was that? Oh right, you're incapacitated. Guess that is how you should have stayed our entire fucking relationship *and* marriage. But guess what else? I'm done. We're over. Here's your phone to call someone who cares and I'm *fucking leaving*!" Kyla walked further into the bedroom to grab Rochelle's phone from the TV stand.

The bedroom door slowly opened more, letting additional light into the dimly lit room. Kyla stopped in front of the TV, holding her wife's phone. Her back was to Rochelle. All Kyla could hear was slithering and dripping, like bare feet squishing through mud or a pot of thick chili slowly starting to bubble.

Kyla turned to look at her wife, the sinister smile changing to an upturned, disgusted frown. Most of Rochelle was a seething emission oozing with saliva-like liquids excreting from her upper chest down to what used to be her toes. Rochelle wriggled slowly back and forth, left to right, exposing the thick mucus fastening her body to the mattress.

Kyla watched in terror as Rochelle's eyes widened and her pupils blackened, becoming plate-sized and docile. The only thing left that looked human was Rochelle's face and shoulders.

"What the fuck..." Kyla pondered out loud.

Thick strings of a tar-like substance shot out from Rochelle's mid-section and grabbed the back of Kyla's neck, shoving her face into the acidic puddle that had once been her wife's kneecaps. Kyla immediately tried lifting herself from the bed, but her face burned and seared with pain. The thick substance coated her face and ricocheted her body right back to the bed.

The sludge covered Kyla's chest and belly, and she reached her arms out to pick herself up, using the bed as leverage. Doing so, pulled her skin from her face, exposing what little tissue was left. One of her eyes popped from its socket. Her blood mixed with the discharge creating more of a pool of gunk on top of Rochelle.

Kyla's eye met with where Rochelle's. The rest of her skin burned like acid, she was still able to watch Rochelle morph into the sick, bitch creature she truly was. Kyla tried to back away, but her own skin melted off, allowing the pain to cease as her nerve endings became non-existent.

Rochelle's face stayed locked on Kyla the entire time. Expression-less for the most part, but watching, nonetheless.

"*You...fucking...bitch!*" Kyla let out her last words loudly and proudly. She lifted what was left of one of her arms, elbow pointed back and high, and clocked Rochelle right through her face.

Kyla's fist sizzled when it punched through a wall of teeth and dredge, hitting the pillow behind her wife's head. Her knuckles squished whatever had been left inside of Rochelle's face.

The pus, mucus, and tar climbed Kyla's forearm melding the two lovers together, like a coiling snake wriggling in bed on a cold, winter night.

The Tale of Norma Wilkes

T ommy and Jake sprinted in front of me. They typically did this and as much as it pissed me off, I'd give them a minute or so before I put on my scolding Aunt voice. Dozens of times they had been here—and they're usually good kids compared to most of the other little shits in the neighborhood. I'd rarely take them this far "off the path," but I can't coddle or shelter them as much as their parents do.

"Hey! Do you both have shit in your ears?! I said *stop*!"

And right before I got the word out of my mouth, Tommy stood dead in his tracks, Jake right behind him. Simultaneously they kneeled to the ground with their backs toward me. The old Wilkes' house only a few feet away, I could only assume what was directly in front of their faces.

"Aunty Ruth, it's a black cat!!!"

"Thank you, Narrator Jake." The years of smoking finally caught up to me, but I caught up to them.

Tommy stood up and just stared at the mansion of a house. Most of the windows had been boarded up with wooden planks—cracked and starting to rot. The house itself looked dark and dilapidated. But I remembered it always looking that way. Jesus Christ, even the front door still had that tiny little entrance for cats to come and go. I half expected bats to fly out of the roof. It was picturesque of a haunted house or some cheesy Halloween gag.

Jake was still petting the cat. Tommy turned to me.

"Aunt Ruth? I think we're old enough now, where you can tell us what *actually* happened here. I mean, *c'mon*, we visit every summer and hear all the older kids talk. But *you* know what *actually* happened. *Right?*"

Before I could answer—or make some sort of excuse—the black cat became suddenly uninterested and ran up the gravel driveway toward the house. The three of us watched him prance away, only to see a gray and black striped cat sitting on the front porch. What was striking, were his green eyes. And those eyes watched us. Then watched the black cat. And then watched us. Making sure of something...

"You think there's more?" Jake was annoyingly inquisitive.

"Probably. I mean...who knows! Pizza for dinner, yes?"

Jake shared my enthusiasm, and we started walking back home. Tommy stared at the house again. I turned to yell, but he swung around, then ran to catch up to us.

The striped cat was now in the third-floor window. The one window jagged with broken, stained glass. He almost looked like a tiger. Staring. Watching.

———————

"All right, Aunt Ruth. This is the perfect time."

While Tommy chewed his pizza and I poured my wine, Jake got comfortable on my couch. *Well, anything to get them to fall asleep early, I suppose.* I grabbed another slice, trying to be as creepy as possible...

"AHHHH HA HA HA HAAAA! HEEEERE BE THE TALE OF NORMA WILKES! WIDOWER AND CAT LADY! TRAINER OF THE TIGERS! PROTECTOR OF THE JEWELS! GUARDIAN OF THE RICHES!!!" I even flicked the table light on and off.

The boys were just too old to fall for my childish story telling skills.

"Come onnnn, Aunt Ruth. There was a giant safe, wasn't there? And she's dead now! Haunting her house for all eternity!"

"Grow up, Tommy. There's no such things as ghosts. Or houses with giant safes..."

Looking back, however, I wasn't sure if I was lying to my nephews or to myself. So, I chugged my wine and got down to brass tacks.

———————

"Everyone in town knew Norma Wilkes was horrid. And it came to no surprise that Henry, her husband, died mysteriously. Sure, they were old. But Norma was such a bitch in public, how could anyone not think she was just as horrid, if not worse, behind closed doors?

"The few times Henry would come to stores by himself for cat food, he always looked defeated. When they came together, she was not only rude to shopkeepers, but she was just as awful to her own husband. Always belittling him in public. But for whatever reason, he just took it.

"She also absolutely loathed *children. Whenever she saw one, she'd stick her nose up—quite literally—and just pretend they were not there. Unfortunately, she had so many damn cats, it drew neighborhood children to their end of the street. She'd yell at the kids, "Get off my property!" Even if they weren't* really *on her property.*

"When Henry died, you would have thought it would have made the evening news. Everyone *knew he had passed. But no one knew* how. *There was a single hearse that showed up at Norma's house. It's only rumored that she was caught yelling at the driver. At least, your Uncle Doug, had always sworn that's what he saw. He was always keeping watch with his idiot best friend, Jack.*

"Jack lived right down the street from here. Each house on opposite sides of the Wilkes' place. Doug and Jack would always argue that the day of Henry's funeral, she was crying, walking to the hearse. Or yelling at the driver.

According to Doug and idiot Jack, there were occasionally visitors at the Wilkes' place. The assumption was that they were relatives or even detectives. Maybe even lawyers. Norma would curse them out and turn them away at the door. And if she happened to not be home, the two green-eyed, striped cats would chase the random visitors away..."

"Aunt Ruth? How would two cats chase anyone away? I mean...they're just cats! It's not like huge barking dogs or anything!"

"I don't know, Tommy. Why don't you ask Uncle Doug?"

Jake stared at me then at Tommy.

"But, Aunt Ruth, Uncle Doug is dead..."

Tommy, being the older one, put his arm around Jake.

"You're right," I continued. "So can I finish?"

"Yeah!"

Both Jake and Tommy grabbed another slice. I poured some more wine, starting to feel a sense of regret and sadness I hadn't felt in years.

"Soon after Henry's death, Norma was seen in town more often. Clearly, she had to run errands on her own. What was strange, according to Doug and Jack, is that Norma was buying an abundance of cat litter and what looked like ground beef by the bulk every other week. Everyone knew she had a lot of cats. But of course, Doug and Jack—being the bored, nosey delinquents they are—decided to take it upon themselves and see if any of the rumors about Norma were true. Now, I, being a few years younger than Doug and Jack, wanted to follow them around. It was summer, and back in those days, in a small town, we had no curfew. There were no 'bad elements' but us kids wandering around.

"*Norma would typically show up at Burt's Grocery every Wednesday in the late afternoon. Doug and Jack would watch her buy the same things. Cat litter. Meat. Cat litter. Meat. So then one day, they decided to follow her home. She'd drive Henry's old Volvo; they'd go on their bikes. They also knew to keep their distance because of her disdain for children. It was planned out perfectly, especially since the sun was setting. And if they just got close enough before she drew her curtains, they'd be able to count each and every cat she has. And maybe even see her open the door to her 'vault full of riches.'*

"*Doug and Jack cycled up behind Norma and waited about ten minutes. They watched her go in the house, turn on the lights and see the ocean of cats from outside march through the front door. There had to be at least twenty of them. But that was the least of their concern. They wanted to get closer to the house. So they did.*

"*The driveway was gravel, same as it is now. And since Doug and Jack have such big mouths about their clockwork plans, I snuck behind them as they had followed Norma. Mom—Grandma—was too occupied with baby Cassie—your guys' mom—at home. Dad—Grandpa—had been working overtime. So even if it was later than normal, no one at home would notice we were both gone.*

"*Doug and Jack were smart enough to walk up to the house, avoiding the noisy gravel. The sun was setting and the late-night summer sky began to darken. And there wasn't a person in sight or a noise to hear from a mile away. Doug always said, 'Livin' somewhere where nothin' happens means there's always somethin' happenin.' But that doesn't mean they didn't notice me right behind them.*

"*There were so many overgrown bushes, that my young mind assumed you couldn't see much from the house to the end of the driveway, into the street. My young mind also didn't realize that Norma's cats were basically guard dogs. At least that's what I eventually told myself.*

"I watched my brother and Jack sneak around the house. They were apparently trying to get a better look inside. But to what? I wanted to see what they were seeing. I kept watching as Doug lifted Jack by his legs to peer into a window. I snuck around to the right of another bush, next to the driveway. I was half way to the house when stupidly *my foot stepped on the gravel.*

"Now, I know it couldn't have been that loud, but the crunch of the rocks as my foot turned echoed, and I thought the noise would alert the entire town of my presence. Within half a second, the noise caused Doug to drop Jack to the ground and they noticed me—in between the bush and driveway—trying to get back behind the bush, when suddenly there were two striped cats. Both with green eyes..."

"Striped cats with green eyes?" Jake again, being annoyingly inquisitive.

"Yes. Gray and black. Why?"

"Just like the one we saw today! Right, Tommy?" He turned to Tommy who suddenly had popcorn.

My wine glass was empty again.

"Jacob, c'mon, this was a long time ago, it's not the same cat we saw today." Tommy explained this to his younger brother while I rolled my eyes and refilled my glass. "*Plus*! We only saw one striped cat. Duh!"

"Well, isn't that just weird, *Thomas*?"

I laughed at them and their cute, sibling relationship. Cassie had done right by them. I had never had a relationship with her like that and she didn't remember Doug. So, I always questioned why she'd even let her sons come here. But then I remembered *she* doesn't remember.

"Should I stop, or are you babies thirsty for more?"

"Well, Aunt Ruth," Tommy, in his older wisdom, continued, "are you gonna tell us what really happened or what?"

"Yeah, Aunt Ruth! Yeah, Aunt Ruth!" Jake, cheering on his older brother, once again.

"Well, all right. But if you keep interrupting and hogging the popcorn, you won't hear about...*the murrrrderrrr*!" I stopped and looked them dead in their eyes.

They knew at this point I was serious, because they had heard the rumors. The ghost stories. The cat stories. They'd heard Cassie mention certain things when she and I talked about the past.

"You know, I talked to Norma once," I admitted, and Jake's eyes widened.

"When Doug and Jack spotted me, I could barely make out their faces. The dim lights from Norma's windows shone just enough for me to see how pissed both of them were. I shrugged at them, and it was the point of no return. They slowly realigned themselves to try and get a peek in the window again. But the damn striped cat who "caught" me decided to make a bother.

"As I tried to sneak further up to my brother, the cat swatted at my bare leg with what I swear at the time were razors, and I fell on the gravel with all my weight. I looked up, about to brace myself, my hand grasping each and every rock of the driveway, the cat hissed and snarled.

"Comically enough, Doug and Jack fell back down to the ground from only seconds of looking through Norma's window. However, this time, no one could be pissed. Everyone had to run. I'm not sure what was scarier: the fact that Norma was yelling inside the house—her voice was mean *and loud—or the snarling of that striped cat. The further I got away, I swear it became almost a howl. A growl. A beast-like noise I will never forget until the day I die.*

"'You fucking idiot!'

Nearing the end of the driveway, I looked back at Doug insulting me. Jack right behind him. And I swear I saw the growling cat inside.

Hissing at us from one of the side windows. A growl that loud from inside? Its eyes greener and bigger.

"'What the hell is wrong with you?'

"We ran all the way home. It was dark that night, too. No moon in the sky to light the way. I only remember because it was the same night I had to catch my breath while defending myself against my brother in the dark.

"'I just wanted to see what you guys were going to see, Doug!'

Jack, I had assumed, said screw this and went back to his house. I thought Doug was going hit me, but he had this odd, determined look on his face. Odd, determined and with a pinch of fear. I'll never forget that either."

Tommy and Jake stared wide-eyed, literally on the edge of their seats.

"Well?"

"Yeah, *well*? What happened next?"

I figured both boys might be bored or even tired. Good thing I never had any kids, these two sure can be annoying with all the questions.

"Look you guys. It's even later now. How about I finish the story tomorrow. I know I'm already going to catch shit from your mother if she finds out I'm telling you all of this."

"How about we finish the story tonight, and all we'll tell Mom is that you swear from time to time?" Tommy, again being annoying in his negotiations.

"All right, fine. But no more interruptions. And go grab your favorite aunt the other bottle of wine in the kitchen."

"Doug and Jack continued their usual adolescent shenanigans throughout the beginning of summer. I, however, learned from my mistake that one night in Norma's driveway and didn't...usually...follow them. Doug would come in late at night, but back then parents didn't

really care. Or have anything to worry about, that is. Mom and Dad were so busy with the baby, the summer was really our babysitter. Free to roam the world with our friends on our bikes. But one day, I did follow Doug and Jack again. Jack showed up around lunch time at our house and I remember this because we were just finishing up those awful bologna and mustard sandwiches Mom made us in between Cassie's crying fits.

"'Bye LOSER!' As soon as Doug saw Jack, he bolted out of the kitchen with dramatic urgency.

"So, with the drama, naturally I had to know what was going on and I snuck up to the window that overlooks the lawn where we'd park our bikes. Doug and Jack were whispering. As they turned their backs to me, Jack pulled something out of his backpack, and Doug jumped back a little. Jack smacked him on his arm and all I wanted to do is know what it was and what the hell they were saying. The damn window was closed. I figured I could go out through the back and follow them again. Like the ninja I thought I was.

"Throwing the rest of the sandwich in the trash, I bolted through the house and out the back door. As the door slammed, I stopped in my tracks, almost yelling Fuck! I didn't need them to hear that or me. I waited a few seconds then poked my head around the house.

"Jack had already started to leave, and as soon as Cassie was screaming crying again, that was the perfect distraction while I snuck out, and Doug scrambled to get on his bike and catch up to Jack. Once they were out of eyesight, I grabbed my bike and walked it on foot to get a glimpse in which direction they were going. A right out of the driveway, a left onto Robinson, then they cut through the Millers'. I know where they were going all right. 'The Wasteland.'

"Lots of kids would hang around The Wasteland because it was near the river—far enough away where not a lot of people went, but close

enough to go and do stupid shit then still be home for supper. I only went there a few times, mostly to eavesdrop, as the older kids would go and smoke cigarettes or do whatever else they did there. This time though, I had a weird feeling, especially with how my brother looked at his best friend a few minutes ago.

"*I made sure to stay a few minutes back but found the main trail most of the kids use. I walked my bike halfway through because I wasn't about to give myself up this time. When I realized I was further down the trail than I had normally been, I spotted Doug and Jack's bikes up against a tree a few feet away, off from the trail. I figured I would back up a bit but keep my bike on the trail, when* bam!

Bam! Bam! Ting!

Bam bam ting! Bam ting!

"*Following the sound, I watched Doug and idiot Jack, who were shooting at cans. They were close to the river, so I was hoping the running water would muffle my footsteps through the shrubs and grass in between the shots. I knew they'd beat me if they saw that I was there, following them again. Luckily, there was a big enough tree I hid behind to watch and listen. One of the perks of being a kid is that you're little. And know how to hide. When you're smart enough, you know how to hide, then escape. I always had a plan.*

"'*I don't know about this, J. Are you sure you saw what you saw? The house is huge anyway. How do you expect this to be so in-and-out like you say?' Doug asked.*

"'*Look man, don't be a pussy. All we have to do is get her to open the damn safe. Henry is dead. The old bat is by herself with a bunch of cats. In and out. No one has to get hurt.'*

"*Doug took the gun from Jack and reloaded.*

"'*Plus, we're just doing this as a uhh...precaution. You know? Just in case.' Jack was always so sure of himself. He handed Doug back the gun.*

'Now do some more. We should be ready for anything. In-and-out, D, in-and-out!'

"*My brother shot a few more times.* Bam! Ting. Bam! Bam! Ting.

"*'Alright, man. But if tomorrow night gets fucked, it's our funeral.'*

"*As I listened, all I could think was, what is idiot Jack getting him into?*

"*Jack took the gun from Doug.* Bam! Ting. Bam! Ting. Bam! Ting. *'Bitch isn't gonna be able to do a damn thing.'*

"*I waited for Jack to reload and start shooting before I got outta there. It was still early afternoon, hot as hell and I didn't need them looking back and seeing me run. All I know is that I had a bad feeling, sweaty skin, and a thousand new mosquito bites. As soon as I heard* bam, *I slowly backed away, with my eyes locked on the backs of their heads. Mostly Jack's though. If he saw me, who knows what he'd be capable of, knowing that I heard every damn word they said.*

"*As soon as I was out of their eyesight, I booked to it to my bike. I pedaled back up the trail like my life depended on it. I figured they wouldn't be back home for a couple of hours, as long as they didn't know I was there. I was scared. I was scared for my brother. I coughed up the dust from the dirt trail as I inched closer and closer to the Millers'. Then back on to Robinson. Then back to our street. Then back to Mom and Dad's.*

"*Jack was always a piece of shit. I knew it then, but it became much clear at this moment. It was always his ideas that got him and my brother into trouble. As young as I was when all of this happened, I'd like to think I was smart for my age, at the time at least. Just...not as smart as I should have been. And I'll pay for that until the day I die.*"

Tommy raised his hand, while Jake looked like he was about to pass out. Tommy noticed and nudged him with his elbow.

"Aunt Ruth...what do you mean? Pay for what?"

Jake awoke to Tommy's question. "Aunt Ruth...what happened next?"

"Well. This will be the end of the story. You both gonna be able to handle it or do you want me to find you some pacifiers so you can both go to sleep?"

"*Nooo!*" they said in unison.

"All right, well...here it is."

"*All I could think about that night was my brother's conversation with Jack. I should have just talked to Doug. I should have just ratted myself out. Maybe the outcome would have been different. Instead, I laid awake all night and stayed quiet the next day doing my ninja thing. Until Doug left in the middle of the night.*

"*It was late. Mom and Dad were gone to Grandma's for the night with Cassie. That was why Doug chose to do it now, I suppose. I heard his bedroom door open and his big feet sneak down the hallway. When he got down the stairs, I saw the faint light of Jack's bike. Like, what the fuck were they doing? I should have done something then, too. I should have called Mom and Dad. I should have tried to reason with Doug. Even make an attempt to tell his friend to piss off. But I was so young. So little. So, I hid. Then I followed.*

"*It was dark. But I watched Doug follow Jack on his bike. They each had a flashlight and what looked like duffel bags. They took a left out of the driveway. Instead of grabbing my bike at first, I watched to see where they were going. Up our street. Down the hill. Then a right on Everett. And up the hill. Now I know where they were going. They were going to Norma's. They were going to rob Norma because they believed all the stories about her being rich and hoarding her dead husband's estate.*

"*I left my bike on the street this time and walked slowly up Norma's driveway. Then one of her cats spotted me. All I could see was a set of gold, glowing eyes. They stopped me dead in my tracks. I could feel the* fear balling up into a pit in my stomach. Though the cat didn't appear to be aggressive, it just stood there and watched as I remained frozen.

"I put a leg out to take a step and as soon as I put my foot down, the cat ran away, up toward the house. Norma's driveway looked fifty miles long—maybe because I was a kid or maybe because it was pitch-black. Nothing but the halfmoon and lights from a few of Norma's windows. And more and more of those reflective gold eyes at the top of the driveway. There had to be at least a dozen sets. Were they warning each other of me? Or of something else?

"As slowly as I could, I made it up the driveway, the gravel pissing me off with each slow step I took. It was like mini air horns underneath my feet, just trying to alert everyone in the neighborhood that I was there. But that wasn't the case. The gravel was just letting the cats know. The closer I got to the house, the more I heard music playing. And when I saw Doug and Jack's bikes behind a bush up against Norma's front porch, I just became more confused. Why in the hell would there be music playing—especially if they already made it inside?

"A part of me just wanted to book it down the driveway, get on my bike and back into my bed. Fuck them. Whatever they were doing, they would probably just get what's coming to them. But I had to know their end game. I went up to one of the windows while two almost identical gray and black striped cats watched me. One stayed on the front porch just staring while the other one went in through the 'doggy door.' I was terrified. And also pissed because the blinds on the window just barely let me see through. Regrettably, barely was just enough.

"'Look bitch. Just open the safe and we won't have to cold cock you again!' Jack was yelling.

"Doug had his gun pointed to Norma, but he just kept looking at Jack's black eyes as he continued to yell. Norma's eye was purple with bruising and swelled shut, even though Jack promised Doug that he *would hold back until they got what they wanted. None of this was in the fucking plan. Neither were all of these cats.*

"'Bro. Just calm down. She'll do it.' Doug got on his knees and in Norma's face. 'RIGHT?!'

"But she just kept crying. The louder she sobbed, the louder Jack would turn up the music. The angrier Jack became with things not going their way, the more Doug became worried.

"'D, just tie her up. We're going to drag her to it ourselves.'

"'All right, J.'

"While Jack put his gun to her head, Doug grabbed duct tape and hiking rope from his pack. Slapping the tape over her mouth and binding her wrists, they pulled her from the floor and brought her into another room.

"The striped cat still staring at me from the porch, still, I walked around it to find the next window.

"There was another window with no light shining through. I kept trying to cover my tracks like a 'Peeping Tom,' on each window I tried. But I had a 'Peeping Tom' of my own—that striped cat. Every time I turned my back, the cat would be there. Just sitting and watching. I never even realized it was walking or following me. It would just be there. At each window. And at each stop I made. I had only forgotten the cat's green eyes when I noticed them on the porch, because in the dark they were that reflective, gold color.

"'Ahhhhhhhhhhhhhhhhhhhhhhhhhhhh!'

"The cat ran away and I almost followed it. Norma. Shit, what were these idiots doing now? I propped myself up at the dark window and was able to get a peek. The window was to a bedroom off of a hallway. And lucky me, a mirror in that hallway showed just enough of Norma, Doug. and Jack. I couldn't see much but all of their backs. And Norma's bloody head.

"'Dude. *Maybe we should just give up, eh? This was all a mistake and the old bat isn't going to give in, even after a few square hits to the face.*'

"'D, we ain't stopping 'til payday is here. Hey! Norrrma! You won't open the fuck thing for us? Well, how about open it for one of your dead cats!'

"Before Norma could open her mouth, Jack fired his gun. Bam! Bam! (No ting) Bam! Between Norma's scream, the shots fired, the awful song playing, my ears ringing and heart pounding, I knew what that asshole did. Because I saw the blood splatter on the mirror.

"Jack grabbed Norma by the feet and dragged her to the end of the hallway. Where the safe was. This wasn't just a safe. It was a vault. As I was trying to gather myself, my thoughts, my conscience, and whatever logic my child-self had, I turned around. No cat. Or cats. No golden eyes in the background. None around the corner of the house, the porch, or down the driveway. Nowhere. Jack didn't kill all 200 of them. Did he? It was my turn to be the idiot. I pried the dark window open. I don't remember why or how, but I did. All of the ongoing commotion in the house must have masked the noise from me opening the creaking the window because I got inside, unnoticed.

"Norma's scream echoed throughout the house. When I peeked my head down the hallway from that bedroom, I saw it. Three dead cats. One all black, one orange and white. And one black and gray striped. With green eyes. I wanted to yell and cry, but the adrenaline was pumping and I was probably in shock. There was blood everywhere. The cats hardly looked like cats—just mangled, furry bodies covered in blood.

"I felt sick. Not even just because of the cats, but because I knew this wasn't going to end well. And I knew I had to get my brother out of this somehow. I followed Norma's cries down the hallway. Her shrieking muffled Jack's words, but in between her sobs I could hear him yell, 'Open it! Just fucking open it!' The hallway felt miles long. Each step I took, *there seemed to be another dead cat. The poor, blood-soaked bodies just further enraged and motivated me to get to my brother. And even to Norma.*

"The light from the part of the house the others were in shined just enough to show each and every blood splatter that idiot Jack created—each little life he took to fuel his greed. And it scared me. The black floors with pools of crimson puddles mirrored from the light's reflection and reflected the walls with each individual splatter for each cat. I felt like I was in a tunnel of death, but death was still at the end.

"I stopped and looked down at my sneakers. They weren't white anymore. They were soaked in the death. Soaked in the blood of all of Norma's cats. This was the point of no return, however. I thought to myself at that exact moment, I could just turn around the way I came and no one would ever know! I could run back down the hallway, find the room, jump out the window and back onto my bike and sneak back into bed and just have years of therapy leaving Doug on his own.

"But I didn't do that."

Tommy and Jake just stared at me, more wide-eyed than I had ever seen.

Fuck. Maybe I made a mistake telling them. Damn wine! Damn cat.

"So, what *did* you do Aunt Ruth?"

And like a cliché, both of them pulled the blankets closer to their faces. I laughed a little because of it, but when they noticed my smile, I think they became even more disturbed.

"I started to think, what if Jack and Doug see me? Will Jack blow me away like these cats? Just from hearing him...He was obviously at the point of no return. The more and more blood I saw, the more and more dead cats I saw in this tunnel of terror, I felt logic and clarity leaving my body. What little bit I had left...All I knew is that I needed to get to my brother. I—quietly—dropped to my knees and crawled the last few

feet of the wretched hallway. Norma's shrieking was getting louder and louder, and I was getting closer and closer.

"'Look, bitch! We are right here! Just open it, and we'll leave you alive with whatever cats you have left!'

"Norma just kept sobbing. In between her cries and yelling, all I could make out was that she couldn't open the safe.

"'Just take what you see in the house. Whatever it is you think is in there isn't. *Just take what you want and go!' Then Norma stopped crying. She looked up and stared Jack right in his face.*

"I saw the back of her head, matted wet with sweat and blood.

"'J, let's just grab a few things and get the hell *out of here. You are fucking us. You are fucking* me.*' And as soon as my brother finished his sentence, he saw me poking my face out from the hallway.*

"Fuck. And just as I thought I was going to get my brother killed, he turned to Jack and pistol-whipped him in the head. Hard. *And I mean* hard. *Jack's skinny ass fell with a loud* thump. *I thought he was dead. But then Norma started screaming again, which meant hell was continuing to break loose.*

"The end of the hallway was no longer my front seat to the shit show. I stood up and came out of the darkness, looking like a crazed, bloodied little girl—according to the mirrors to the right of the room. They reflected not only the safe, Norma, Jack, and Doug...but me. My hands and legs were covered in the blood and shit I trudged through to get to them all.

"'Ruthie? What the fuck are you doing here?' Doug ran over to my enamored self.

"I couldn't believe what I saw in the mirror, I couldn't believe anything that happened in this house. But what I do know, is that I made it to my brother.

"'We should go, Doug.' I could hardly get the words out of my mouth. I put out my hand to his.

"I swear, he went to grab mine, but my palm got sprayed with something. And my ears were ringing. And Doug's chest was bleeding from the inside out. He dropped to his knees and I was so confused because blood was pouring out of his mouth. What did I do? All I could do was stare at his eyes staring back at mine. As he dropped to the floor, I wanted to yell louder than Norma. Then I looked up and saw Jack's finger on the trigger.

"Now, when you hear about people talking about things happening in slow motion, it doesn't just happen in the movies. When you hear about people fainting or blacking out, that happens too. Because when I watched my brother drop dead and saw Jack behind him, Norma was already opening the safe. The vault. What ran out came for all of us. Fight or flight? What we choose can literally define us.

"It went after Jack first. I had always thought this happened because the monster knew Jack was an awful human being. But realistically, it was just proximity. Norma had opened the vault door with what little strength she had left but was out of sight when she released her beast. Jack turned around just to see the last thing he would ever see.

"The animal leapt toward Jack's scrawny body, pinning him to the floor, just to eat his face. Its eyes were yellow, fur onyx black. Fangs and claws thick and sharp like rows of machetes. This was the time I blacked out. Or maybe everything was still going in slow motion? Blood and flesh spewed from the beast's mouth with every deep, hungry bite. Jack tried to scream, but all that came out was a muddled, horrifying gurgle—until his jaw was broken, ripped off, then spat on the floor of Norma's now House of Horrors.

"That's when I actually blacked out. The sound. The sound of his jaw breaking.

"*The initial shock, then more shock, must have awoken my adrenaline back to life because I remembered there was a gun or two strewn about somewhere. Between Norma crying and screaming, Jack being eaten alive, and my brother's dead body lying on the ground right in front of me, I knew this was it. The moment of truth. The moment that would either kill me, or define me. And in what seemed like nanoseconds, I spotted the gun not too far from me. On the floor, in between where I stood and Jack being feasted on. Norma was hiding behind the vault door.*

"*I quickly grabbed the gun. Thinking that the beast wouldn't notice my normal stealthy—or clumsy—self, but it did. I started to step back but all I could seem to do was focus on Jack's missing face. Just a gaping, bloody, hollowed-out skull.*

"*Up until these last few hours, I hadn't really thought about death too much. Certainly not the macabre that can come with it. But all of these thoughts, the pounding of my heart hard against my chest, and heavy breaths were stopped dead in their tracks...when the giant animal stopped chewing and looked right into my eyes. Playing with Jack's body was just an appetizer. The slower I stepped away, the faster it got closer to me. I was so terrified, I almost forgot I was holding the gun.*

"'*Hey!' Norma yelled, coming out from behind the vault door. She was holding a cattle prod. It was red on the end.*

"*I remember it being red because it matched the blood on her face and head. It matched the entire room, in fact.*

"*Somehow, her voice startled the animal and it backed down. It whimpered as its ears curled back. Norma got closer to me—and it—and I fell on my ass. The beast backed away a few steps. Norma stood above me, beaten and bleeding, looking like an old, evil witch that likes to throw children in her oven.*

"*She pointed the cattle prod at me, 'Is there anyone else in my house?'*

"'No.'

"I fought back tears, trying to ignore how cold my body felt. Norma's glare gave me shivers, and I could feel the hatred and anger coming from her. I wanted to plea, I wanted to say, 'Hey lady, this ain't my fault.' But I couldn't. We were both blood-soaked, having a staring contest. Until she lifted her fingers to her mouth.

"Her fucking whistle echoes in my head every now and then, 'til this very day.

"I don't know why I assumed she was going to help me. She was just going to feed us all to the beast, like the bitch that she is. Because that was Norma Wilkes.

"But Norma Wilkes must not have seen that I grabbed the gun.

"As soon as the whistle left her lips, the beast lunged toward me. I aimed, shot, and as it roared out in pain, I quickly got up to target Norma. I knew one shot was not going to keep the animal down for long. Shit, I didn't even know where I hit it. I stared at Norma, looked at the dreaded hallway, knowing it was my only escape. Back the way I came. Her and I met eyes for the last time and just as I was about to pull the trigger for a warning shot, a gust of wind brushed past my face. That's when I started running.

"Back down the hallway of horrors. My sneakers slid across the blood-ied floor, all while trying not to trip on the poor, dead cats. I wasn't even thinking about my brother and his idiot friend. The sounds of Norma's screams, the beast's growling and chewing was deafening. Managing to not fall again...

"Norma being torn apart gave me just enough time to take that right, jump across the room like a super hero, then out the window.

"I stood up against the house in an attempt to compose myself and figure out my next move. The muffled sounds of screaming dissipated, as I realized I was still clutching the gun and shaking. My eyes started *to tear up because I realized my brother is dead. I'm covered in blood and holding the gun that shot a giant beast, all while Norma Wilkes is surely cat food.*

"Dropping to the ground, trying to gather my thoughts, I heard footsteps on the gravel driveway. Did it get out? Just as I was surely about to yell out profanity, I knew I hardly had the strength to pick myself up and run more. But then I looked up. It was the other striped cat. With green eyes. Now I just started to feel even worse, and his brother's blood was probably somewhere on me.

"A few more cats popped out. They didn't come as close as he did, but I could see a few pairs of glowing eyes in the dark. I put my hand out to the striped one, he sniffed it, gave me a lick, and walked away. The eyes slowly disappeared into the dark and I took that as permission to finally get the hell out of there.

"I found myself back home, debating on calling for Mom and Dad. Then I remembered they took Baby Cassie to Grandma's for the weekend. Showering, trying to forget the trauma and wash the blood from my hands...literally...my young mind convinced itself to bury the gun and bloodied clothes, then crawl into bed."

I was about to conclude the story with the days and weeks that followed, when I was interrupted by Tommy's snoring and Jake's drooling on my couch. They were passed out. I guess they had enough. Frankly, so had I. Going down Memory Lane was never my favorite trip to make. I chugged my last glass of wine and slept as soundly as my nephews were.

Maybe it's true what writers say. Story telling can be just as terrifying as it is cathartic. All at once.

It was just before dusk the next day when Cassie showed up to bring Jake and Tommy back home. I waved goodbye to their smiling faces.

The dust from her car driving off began to settle, and I felt myself staring down the street.

Up the street, down the hill, right on Everett. Aside from walking by Norma's house with Jake and Tommy, I had vowed to never go near there ever again. Beginning to question staying at Mom and Dad's house after they died—and questioning life in general at this point—I found myself walking up the street. And going down the hill. And taking that right on Everett.

With all these cats, I assumed whatever animals had survived that night had been left to fend for themselves and just kept having kittens, never really leaving. Generations of cats and years had gone by, yet they still frequented this vacant, ugly house.

When my feet hit the gravel driveway, I turned into that curious, scared little girl. *What the hell am I doing?* I walked up to the front door—I think for the first time—and put my hand to a giant dent. *This must have been when the cops showed up.*

Stupidly, I tried the door knob, but they must have dead-bolted it from the inside out. *You're a dumbass, Ruth. Just call it a day and get the hell out of here.* But when I walked back down the rotting steps of the porch, a black cat ran by, around the corner of the house.

Must have been the one we saw the other day. Let me just double-check, because I sure as shit don't believe in ghosts.

I almost didn't recognize the window behind the growth of all the unkempt grass and bushes. The very same window that almost got me killed. And also saved my life.

No black cat, though.

The summer sky was turning from its pink and orange to a dark blue, welcoming the moon with a bright red luminescence. Even though all of the windows were boarded up, the wood from the boards were rotted just like the rest of the house. I ripped off one of the boards and broke a part of the window glass.

The wood was so rotted from the inside too, that the brass lock just sunk in. Little to no effort and I was back in the house. The light the sun had left poured through the streaks of the dirty window. *I could just leave now.* But as I took a few more steps and saw the Hallway of Horror, something inside me said I had to see that room with the vault. I just needed to. I needed to know it all really did happen and I wasn't crazy.

The hallway was pitch black. The faster the sun was setting, the faster it dawned on me that I needed to be able to see. *Duh!* I grabbed my keychain with a tiny flashlight which didn't do much except show an inch or two of what was in front my eyes.

One foot in front of the other. I kept walking and shining the light ahead. To the walls. To the floor. Then in front of me. The walls were covered in a thick blanket of dust and cobwebs. The cobwebs crept down from the ceiling, stretching throughout the hallway like a thick spiderweb waiting to net prey. I saw the dark brown stains on the floor when I got closer to the end.

Obviously, clean-up wasn't the prerogative when they decided to board up and condemn the house after everything happened. I knew what those stains were. The cats that Jack shot. *Jack, you fuck.* My skin felt grimy from all of the dust. My steps, as quiet as I was trying to be, echoed.

Then I got to the end.

I froze when I saw the closed door of the vault. Holding the tiny flashlight to it, my hand shaking, keys jiggling...

Thump!

Just as I was going to shit myself, I saw a pair of those reflective eyes. One of the cats jumped out of nowhere. My flashlight exposed a black and grey striped cat. With green eyes.

"Well, sir, you look *just* like your predecessor."

It took all my strength to hide my fear—or ignore it, rather—as I bent down, with my hand out, to the cat. The little light and all the dark made it hard to tell, but the cat looked not necessarily old...but wise and weary.

He sniffed my hand and licked it. Then ran away. I heard a few other *thumps* and pitter-patters, and assumed it was mice and the other cats that had taken over the abandoned property. I walked toward the vault.

Well, I'm here and might as well open it. I want to know what Norma had been protecting, what she had been quite willing to literally kill—or die—for. When I turned the wheel, I couldn't believe it wasn't locked. But I assumed whoever shut up the house had done so in a rush and had thrown away whatever key, erasing the past.

The door was heavy. Using my whole body, I pulled it as far as it would go. I listened for a minute.

Complete silence, except my heart pounding faster and faster.

The couch that had been there when I was here last, now covered in decades of dust, seemed like the perfect tool to keep the vault door propped open. Every slow step I took, each particle of dust I breathed in and coughed out, just fed my regret of doing this. But I still needed to see what was in there. *Seeing*, being the operative action out of this whole fucking ordeal.

From what I could tell, the floor was mostly cement, with sections of carpeting. The walls, covered in more cob webs, barely hid large, what looked like scratches—from the beast, I assumed. And the smell...Let's just say anyone would be lucky to not recognize what that smell was.

Then, in the corner...a body.

A decades-old skeleton flopped over and broken like an old doll. The watch.

Holy shit, it's Henry Wilkes.

Behind poor Henry, there were dozens and dozens of bodies. All in different forms of decay.

When I got closer to the piles of parts strewn about, I heard something. It was much louder than a pitter-patter or tiny paws on the gravel driveway.

A heavy, slow growl...

I turned my light over to the opposite corner, showing the beast. Its snout and legs gray with age, surrounded by bones, garbage, and other various bits. I was *not* interested in finding out what they all were.

Fuck.

As soon as we locked eyes, I turned and ran. I ran just like I did as a little girl. Fast and clumsy. The cement floor killed my old knees and when I jumped the couch to get back to the Hallway of Horror, I could feel that gust of wind—the beast's breath—mere inches behind me.

I sped out of the cave, through the Hallway of Horror, almost sliding past the room with the window, then dove through the opening like a superhero again. Or maybe just like an older stunt person. The tall, unkempt grass braced my fall, and I lay there for a few seconds in disbelief, kissing the dirt.

There's no way it could follow me out here. I barely fit out the window. Fuck.

It didn't need to fit out the window. Because it just jumped right through it. And it was pissed.

The sun had set, the night sky almost as black as the beast's fur. But I saw the scar on its leg. *Gun shot from me, I presume? There's no talking your way out of this. You're just dead. And I have no gun this time.*

My arms were working just enough to crawl backward, my legs shaking. The beast's yellow eyes saw red—and red was me. Our eyes were locked and as much as I wasn't prepared to die, I didn't want to die like this. I remembered Norma's screams.

Thump!

The striped cat with green eyes jumped in between us. The beast huffed and backed up a bit. They just stared at each other. It felt like hours, the three of us staying there frozen in time. Me...I was rigid with fear. I heard more rustling in the bushes behind me and other little feet on the gravel. But my eyes were focused on the beast.

It sniffed the striped cat, digging its paws in the ground a few times. I knew right then and there it was going to take all of us out. But then something happened.

It lifted its head and smelled the air. His eye dilated and nose twitched. That beautiful summer breeze withered its way through his nostrils. He looked at the sky, looked at the ground and the house behind him. Then he turned and saw more trees adjacent to where we all stood. He must have just had some sort of realization.

The howl that came from his mouth was nothing I'd ever heard before—or since.

The beast walked backward, then turned. And ran around the corner of the house, past the front porch, and out to the woods, into whatever unknown freedom he had never had.

My brain finally processed what had just happened and I pet the striped cat with green eyes.

"I think I'm done here."

The Contest

Maya Powers stood over River's body. She tightened her grip on the microphone and stared at River's bleached strands of hair—once blond, now just red and soaked, making it difficult to decipher where the black roots began and where the blood stopped. Maya wasn't sure if she should feel guilt or pleasure while River Daniels, the "esteemed" author and popular social media presence, convulsed and shuddered.

Blood from the blow to River's head continued to stream out, pouring down to the wooden floor of the backstage and filling in the cracks, like some sick Tetris game. Maya kept one foot on River's abdomen to quiet the convulsing.

Shawn Smith, the third contestant, held his hands to his face in horror. He sat on the cold floor, wondering the same thoughts Maya was, but he seemed just a bit more sympathetic. "Well, what the hell do we do now?" Shawn's voice shook as he tried to hold back tears.

"I...I don't know. But being crucified isn't exactly what I planned," Maya said with confidence. She looked behind her at the curtain that had just been pulled back. "People are still leaving. Shall we run or hide?"

"Well. This is obviously a plan for someone with bigger balls than me."

"Great. Why do I have to do everything?" Maya struck River one more time as hard as she could, and the body's jerking finally stopped.

One Week Earlier

Maya sat in her dingy basement apartment, surrounded mostly by shadows of dim lamp light. She clicked on the email she had been waiting for, closing her eyes, then slowly opening her lids before she reading aloud to herself.

"Ms. Powers, you are officially a finalist in *Word Fusion*'s Poetry Contest. As expected, per the agreement in the submission guidelines, you are invited to a read-aloud with the two other finalists. The panel of judges will then decide who the first place winner is. Please call the following number to confirm your acceptance. The hotel room will be in your name will and require official identification."

Maya couldn't believe it. This was the first writing contest she had ever made traction on. The fact she had a hotel room waiting for her—and *paid for*—was just another bonus she couldn't have ever dreamed of.

Immediately, she signed on to *BookSpace* to share her exciting news. The email didn't indicate who the other two finalists were, but she didn't care. The excitement and pride had her gloating all evening. Maya celebrated in her dark, small home with the social media post and a six pack of her favorite hoppy ale. As the beers kicked in, she ignored the darkness looming in her mind—self-doubt amongst other feelings of dread. Even with good news—*great* news—she still had that sense of impending doom. Ignoring it all, she chugged the last beer and fell asleep, making the near-future plans in her mind before passing out.

The next morning as Maya clocked in for work, her less-than-lucrative remote job, and immediately messaged her manager, explaining she would need a few days off. Luckily, Maya's supervisor, Denise, was supportive. But it wouldn't have mattered if she wasn't supportive because Maya had accrued enough time to take months off at that point. Her technical writing position wouldn't hurt the company if she was away, anyway.

Maya waited for Denise's official approval and slid her rackety office chair to the other side of her desk, checking for messages on *BookSpace*. Her online writer friend Shawn messaged her, congratulating her on becoming a finalist, then a second message of a screenshot containing the same email she had received—but to him! Maya replied with how excited she was and asked if he knew who the other finalist was.

She had been trying to stay off social media for the most part, always finding herself continually scrolling through drama and memes instead of writing. With three books of poetry and a dark fantasy novella under her belt—all of which had a 4.8 rating or better on *ReadGood*—she was starting to have a positive feeling about this contest. The poem that had won her spot on the top three for Word Fusion, titled "I Knew It Was You" was her favorite, which had taken her years to write and finally finish.

Maya went back to actively working. One more day of it. She began to pack early so she was good and ready to leave for the hotel and sweep her beloved online friend and the mystery finalist. Maya pictured accepting the first place award with a permanent smile all morning and afternoon. A smile, in general, was extremely rare for her.

After clocking out from the day job, she stared at her half-packed bags. The inexpensive lamps glowing within the cheap apartment oozed with sadness. Maya tried to stay optimistic, reminding herself even just being a finalist in this contest was a "big deal." She looked toward her walls of books, including her own, and began to give into her natural pessimism.

No one else thinks it's a big deal that I published books. Why should I? If no one else gives me credit for anything, why should I give myself credit for what I've 'accomplished'? Maya stopped herself from packing more clothes.

She plopped down onto her hand-me-down futon, which served as both her bed and seating for company she rarely had, then opened up laptop to see what was going on with everyone else. Her heart felt heavy, watching the *Congratulations!* comments pour in. Thankful for the support of online strangers, Maya realized she hadn't read the replies from Shawn.

"You're never going to fucking believe it—but the other finalist is RIVER. RIVER FUCKING DANIELS. SHE'S BEEN BOASTING ABOUT IT SINCE WORD FUSION MADE THE ANNOUNCE-MENT. I know you deleted her from your profile a while back, but I HAD to tell you. Whatever! Message me when you leave and we can meet up at the hotel bar. LOVE YA, BITCH!"

Maya stared at the message from Shawn. Her heart pounded, and her throat swelled up. The "esteemed" River fucking Daniels. The troll. The book-writing, poem-spewing, dictator of *BookSpace* members. The one, the only, the privileged... *River Daniels.*

Maya messaged Shawn back:

"She's going down. And you and I are going to beat her."

Three Days Prior to the Contest

Maya was able to contain her rage with gleefulness. Checking into the hotel had been seamless, but she still felt a dark cloud looming above her. She was used to the feeling of disappointment—surviving on the day job, scraping by, yet always wondering if what she wrote even mattered. Luckily, the online community felt and shared the same despairs.

Prepared to fake it until she made it, Maya went through the finalist agreements with a fine-toothed comb and practiced how she would read her poem. *That bitch River won't see anything coming.* Maya lost herself in her thoughts once again, messaging Shawn as she walked into her hotel room.

Obviously, the room was more elegant than her apartment. The natural lighting alone stung Maya's eyes. *Clean bedding? A shower bigger than my entire bathroom? I think I can handle this.* Maya was training herself to think positive thoughts for the duration of her stay. She tested out the bed, sitting down and bouncing for the fun of it. Then she decided to text Shawn to see if he was at the hotel yet.

He eventually got back to her saying to meet him at the bar downstairs. Maya showered first, then posted another update on *BookSpace* with pictures of the view from outside her hotel room. She smirked, caught a glimpse of this in the mirror, and began to frown.

What if public speaking is my downfall? What if the judges place me last because of what I'm saying and not what I wrote? What if fucking River Daniels wins first place? The room became darker, matching her thoughts. The *ting* from her phone interrupted her. It was Shawn asking where her ass was.

Maya put her thoughts on the backburner, as always, gathered herself, and found the elevator. Excited to meet up with another online author buddy in person, she stepped out of the elevator and turned the corner toward the glass doors encasing the cheesy yet fitting hotel bar.

She spotted Shawn's profile. His arms were just as vocal as his speaking. He was having a conversation at the bar...with the one and only...River Daniels. Maya slowed her pace, listening in on their conversation from afar. Shawn was always known to be truthful via his social media page but neutral as well. Maya knew he secretly hated

River too, but he hadn't been subjected to a personal attack from her. They also read and reviewed each other's books publicly, so Shawn remained less outspoken "until the time was right."

"Ha! Yes, I mean, I wasn't even going to *accept* this nomination because I heard one of the judges is *against* using pronouns! But once his biracial daughter confirmed on Spectogram that it was just a rumor, I figured, what the hell?" River proclaimed, slightly slurring her speech.

Shawn rolled his eyes at her pretentiousness.

Maya stood back to listen more and watch. River had a boyish face and a small, pointed nose. Maya pictured River's head exploding, ego and brain dripping down like murder scene contents all over the bar, spraying on to Shawn's cheeks.

She shook her head back to reality and focused on River's frizzy hair and its bad dye job. It was like she was trying to look like someone or something other than that who she actually was. Or maybe River just didn't know how to dress or do her own makeup. You'd never know though, with all the selfies she posted on *BookSpace*. Bragging about being at some "job." Adults over the age of thirty-five typically didn't look good with facial piercings either.

But Maya, no stranger to the bias of others, tried not to judge on appearances. She formed her opinion of River based on the other author's ridiculous online antics, which included a deluded sense of self-worth, telling other authors what they should or should not say, as well as being worshipped with cult-like status.

River's virtue-signaling and performative allyship was both obvious and pathetic. She wasn't a good writer; she's a good manipulator. Though it was debatable those might be mutually exclusive, when you're a sheep, you go with the herd. River was their dictator, a blind leader leading the blind.

I'll make her blind. By ripping that cheap metal out of her face and stabbing her eyeballs with it all...

"Holy shit! Maya Powers! You finally made it, Girl!!!" Shawn yelled toward Maya, giving her a look of desperation.

"Shawn! Can you believe it? We're here!" Maya walked up and hugged Shawn disregarding the presence of the third finalist.

River just stared at them both while they conversed without her, and she eventually excused herself. Maya watched River's back get smaller and smaller until she was out of the bar. She imagined herself chasing after River and stabbing her spine with a cocktail stirrer.

One Day Before the Contest

Shawn and Maya sat on the king size bed in his room, taking one last shot of whiskey and airing out their concerns for the reading and the judge panel. "Look," Shawn started to say, "your poem is one of the most relatable, thought-provoking things I've ever read in the last few *years.* So, stop doubting yourself. Just feel it and read it."

"Shawn. Love you. Truly. But neither of us has a chance with River fucking Daniels. For all we know, she's blackmailing the judges by comments they made twenty years ago at a poetry slam with a puppy-mill theme, put on by Native American sympathizers."

"*Hah!*" Shawn let out a few more laughs. He got up from the bed to check his phone for texts from his husband.

Maya fidgeted with his fluffy frog keychain.

"Look, Madam Powers...we could just kill River. But I'd *rather* have the satisfaction of watching her lose this competition. It's *all* she's been posting about on *BookSpace.* Plus, maybe we could sneak a video of her being a complete bitch and post it. She isn't the only one worthy of calling others out on their bullshit." Shawn stared at the half-drank bottle, about to suggest if one more sip would affect their reading capability during tomorrow's contest.

"Ugh. Maybe you're right."

"About one more shot of this whiskey?"

"About killing her."

The Contest

Maya sat upon the stage overlooking an impressive amount of people in the audience. Her chest seared in pain, the anxiety continually creeping inside her head. Her arms and finger tips moist with sweat. Maya clasped her hands tight, then eventually forced a smile and clapped as Shawn eloquently finished reading his poem. She became a little teary-eyed, truly proud of her friend.

The audience and judges mirrored her splendor for Shawn's words. He walked back to the stool next to her and blew out a sigh of relief.

"*We're almost done*!" He mouthed.

River stood up from her seat and walked toward the microphone stand. She waved and even did a pompous little bow toward everyone facing the stage. Maya watched River, but all she could see was red. River started to recite her poem, yet all Maya heard was ringing in both ears. The ringing became louder and louder like a swarm of bees stinging at her eardrums.

Maya visualized herself walking right up to the podium River was speaking at, grabbing River by the jaw, and pulling the bone from her face as hard as she could. She continued to imagine the sound River's face would make. The skin ripping from the muscle, the blood cascading from her ugly face, down to the ground for all to see. Maya pictured the gagging reflex of River's missing jaw and the swarming of people from the audience trying to stop her. Getting one last punch to River's gut...The mist of blood that would dust Maya's face when the people tried to pull her away from the massacre...

"And now...Maya Powers is up! Reading 'I Knew It Was You'"

Maya snapped out of it and started toward the podium. *Stop fucking around woman. You can do this. You can do this.* She looked back at Shawn and he gave her a thumbs up. Maya had always known he'd have her back. She adjusted the microphone on its stand, and cleared her throat.

"I'm Maya Powers. This is titled 'I Knew It Was You...'" Maya looked up from the microphone and stared at the crowd before her.

The silence mixed in with people coughing and fidgeting in their seats. The judges watched her, waiting for her to continue.

"When the sky cracked open

I knew it was you

Because I was able to move

The dark turned to light and the walls shattered down

Imagery meant something again

And I knew it was you

Picking me up when nightmares pushed me down

The horrors persisted

My face just a clown's

The truth-mirror a gift

I knew it was you

When the sky closed up

My scars re-opened

My blood pink then black

Yet your hands another gift

I knew it was you

Healing can be long

Or funny

Or absolutely terrifying

At the base

In the middle or top

Your pedestal not just my foundation

But my entire life

And still

I knew it was you

However

When it all broke

When it all went to shit

My heart never being the same

Or beating at all

Bleeding out

I still

I still knew

I still knew it was you"

Maya looked up again, watching people smile, cry, and clap. The judges wrote their notes and compared with each other. She walked back to her stool, stared at River's dead eyes, then grinned back at Shawn. He was teary-eyed just as she had been earlier.

The head judge said there would be a short intermission, and within half an hour, they would announce the winner. Maya gave Shawn a look, then they went back stage to pace and wonder. It seemed like hours. Maya and Shawn had small talk, but River just stood there, on her phone the entire time, more than likely posting on *BookSpace* about how much better she had read than everyone else on the planet.

"Hey guys! It's time!" The overly enthusiastic host screeched.

Maya looked at Shawn, gripped his hand with a quick squeeze, before the three finalists walked back out on stage to hear what the judges had decided. She was running on adrenaline, surveying the audience, hardly able to decipher what the judges were saying.

"On that note, it is our *pleasure* to announce the winner of Word Fusion's Twenty-First Annual Poetry Contest...RIVER DANIELS!!!"

The audience stood up and yelled in excitement, clapping their hands along with the panel of judges. Maya's throat tightened, and her heart started to slow and burn within her chest. Shawn tilted his head toward River as she walked toward the podium. He then grabbed Maya's hand, noticing it was still holding the microphone.

Present Time

"You don't need bigger balls. Just bigger muscles. Help me with this piece of shit." Maya made her commands and grabbed River's feet.

Shawn hesitated for a second, then stood up. He grabbed River by the shoulders before spotting a dressing room around the corner. "*There!*" he said, quite sure of himself. His normally cute button face was serious.

Maya was surprisingly impressed.

The finalists entered the dressing room, and Maya threw the bottom half of River's body to the floor. Shawn was still holding on. Maya closed the door just enough for her to screen the backstage.

"I don't think anyone else is going to come back here."

She shut the door and watched Shawn carefully place River on to the floor. He then stared at Maya and crossed his arms.

"What?"

"What do you mean, *what*? Maya, you just killed her and you seem less than concerned. I'd rather just check out of the hotel and forget any of this fucking happened."

"Good plan. Let's just leave her ass here and sneak out through the other exit. No one knows where any of us went. They can pin it on an accident or some transient that hangs out in the alley." Maya heard herself speak. She tried to breathe in and out like a normal person, but this was not a normal situation. Maya also thought she did not want her friend to get in trouble for her actions. Her heart started beating faster again, and she looked over to River's eyes.

They were still open.

"I'm going now. And I'd like to never see you again," Shawn continued. "At least, not until the next contest, when *I'm* ready commit murder. By the way...the murder weapon...urr...the microphone is still in your pocket."

Maya looked down. She had forgotten she shoved it in her pants before moving River. Maya backed up, to staring at River's eyes again, only for Shawn to leave the dressing room and shut the door. Her ears were ringing, her head pounded but the migraine seemed to dissipate the closer she got to River's body.

Maya ripped out River's nose ring, yet again surprised at the ease of taking the metal out of flesh. She watched mini streams of blood course from River's nose down to her chin. Maya placed the piece of jewelry in her back pocket then peeked out the dressing room door.

The stage curtain was still drawn, backstage dark, and the gleaming red exit sign out to the alley was clear.

Time to get the fuck out of here. Maya smirked, encompassed in her thoughts and quietly left the auditorium.

Later on, she texted Shawn one word: "Sorry."

Then began to plot a three-part murder mystery series.

Rooms of Terror

Tim was startled awake once again by his wife screaming his name. He sat up and turned to her, placing his hand on her arm. Her skin was wet and cold, like it always was when she had one of her attacks.

"Jade. *Jade*! I'm here. It's okay."

Jade was crying and hyperventilating, but feeling his touch eventually brought her back to reality, calming her breathing. And her heart rate.

"Timothy! Fuck, I thought there was someone at the end of the bed. *Fuck*! I'm...I'm sorry."

"Dear, it's fine. But this keeps happening, and I'm honestly getting pissed off that nothing is helping you. Also...I'm tired too."

Jade steadily breathed in through her nose and felt guilty. Though the tears were drying on her cheeks, the wet dripping from her nostrils continued.

"Look..." Tim flicked on the overhead light. "There is no one in here. And now we're going to go through the entire fucking house to put you at ease."

Jade's eyes adjusted slowly from the pitch-black bedroom—and at her husband who was staring back at her—to the lit-up space. The overhead light, though dimmed, showed their perfectly, normal-looking room. Dresser, TV, nightstands. The closet door slightly ajar revealing shoes on the floor and the hanging wardrobe.

Nothing. It's normal. It looks all normal, Jade thought.

Tim rubbed the crust from his eyes, then stood up. "Okay. Let's do this." He reached his hand out to Jade, who was still sniffling.

She threw the blankets off herself, and clasped his hand. Baxter, the couple's chubby cat, huffed and ran out of the room—something else Jade was used to seeing. All the shrinks, the different drugs...were doing nothing. So, she let Tim guide her through their dark house at 3:17 a.m. to *prove* there was nothing wrong.

Nothing wrong, except maybe her.

Tim opened the bedroom door, exposing the dark hallway.

Jade watched muddied hands grip the doorframe. There were dozens of them. Bloody-knuckled, scabbed, dirt-covered appendages were leaving a trail of crimson and muck sliding back and forth from the hallway to the bedroom opening. The awful sound of fingernails breaking echoed in Jade's head, and the hands dug further and further into the drywall. Bones started to snap, and as the hands attempted to break down the walls...

"See? Look. Nothing." Tim flicked on the hallway light.

Everything was normal again.

Jade blinked a couple of times, looking at Tim and easing her grip on his hand. *How can he not see it? It was just here.*

She remained quiet with her thoughts while Tim led her to the bathroom just down the hallway. Jade started sweating again. Her heart began to pound harder and harder within its anxious state, like it typically did. The hallway light illuminated the glossy floor, and Jade watched her bare feet follow Tim's.

Right before they entered bathroom, Tim's hand slid from Jade's. The rest of his body went with it, into the abyss.

Jade's eyes widened. Her arm still stretched out, waiting for the touch of Tim's hand.

"Timothy?" Hardly getting the whisper out, she slowly walked toward the doorway.

The bathroom door creaked back from her. Her face started to burn, and she began to step into the doorway.

Tim tripped and fell, slamming to the floor with a wet plop. His head poked out on its side, bleeding from his ears and scalp. Jade's stomach turned, preparing for her heart to beat out of her chest. All she could do was freeze and watch her beloved husband's eyes roll back into his head. More blood pooled into his eyelids.

"See? Look. Nothing."

Tim turned the bathroom light on. Jade's mouth was so dry, she was unable to speak.

She should have known he didn't really fall. Jade had pictured his demise hundreds of times. Luckily none of it ever *actually* happening. But it was something she always imagined. Not because she wanted it to, but because she feared a life without him. And those fears always took form.

Jade ran to the sink, blasting the cold water on her face. *The shower though. What about the shower?* She started to drink straight from the faucet.

Tim already knew what she was thinking and pulled back the curtain. An empty tub, everything sparkling clean. "C'mon," Tim commanded in a calm yet stern manner.

Jade wondered how this kind, patient man still continued to put up with a crackpot like her.

These thoughts made her sad. They both left the bathroom, walking to the end of the hall where the office was. About ten steps away,

Jade's sadness turned into something else. She had seen a shadow of a being glide past the office door opening.

Jade stopped in her tracks, unable to swallow. Tim tugged at her hand. He continued to attempt to pull her forward, but the sweat from the bottoms of her feet glued her to the hardwood flooring. Though the hallway light provided some sight into their modest home office, she heard the footsteps of a third person.

"Timothy, it's coming from in there." Jade could hardly get words out. Her tongue felt like sandpaper scraping the roof of her mouth.

The lights suddenly dimmed, blacking out Tim's body. Books from the shelf in the far corner of the office began being thrown into the hallway. The *thump! thump!* sound of each book made Jade's body twitch harder and harder.

Instead of staying frozen this time, she walked toward the office, only to find a masked man holding a rifle.

This is it. A fucking home invasion, she thought.

The window adjacent to the office door was open, and the cool breeze overtook her body. Jade looked directly into the black eyes of the gun-toting figure. Both his hands were full: one with a thick book, the other lifting his weapon, aiming for Jade's chest.

There's nothing anyone can do to prepare themselves for a moment like this. Even if you've imagined it a thousand times. Self-defense doesn't typically kick in when you're having an anxiety attack in your pajamas and the knife you habitually carry isn't in your pocket. Not that it would even help.

The trigger clicked, and the light in the office emphasized the current reality, brightly.

"Jade. *Jade!*"

Tim closed the window in their home office, and the smack of the wood and glass pulled Jade back in. Her pupils, once plate-sized, resumed to normal. So did the lump in her throat.

"Jesus Christ, Timothy. Now what?"

"We're finishing this, dear. I need you to know *and see* there's nothing to be afraid of." Tim once again grabbed Jade's hand to lead her downstairs.

Jade's body temperature rose from corpse-like to an average, living human being. She clasped her chest with her free hand, feeling, to make sure there no bullet had lodged in her chest.

There wasn't.

Jade questioned whether her husband should just check her into a psych ward and leave her to rot. But he led her down the stairs to the rest of the house. Once again, only a part of the stairway was lit up enough for her to see.

Step by step, she gripped Tim's hand, each stair cool and hard. Tim's pace gained, and when Jade tried to catch up, her left foot pushed down on something. Soft at first, then a crunch, like a giant egg cracking beneath her foot. It felt sharp and wet.

"Oh my fucking god, Timothy!" Jade stepped aside on the same step, reaching toward her foot with her right hand. She felt hard chunks and a fur-like substance soaked with tar.

Jade moved further down the stairs, then turned around to look at her hand.

Orange hairs, bone, and blood pierced her palm.

"*Baxter? What the fuck did I do? Baxter?*" Jade looked up the staircase.

Her precious cat had bent and folded between two stairs, not one foot above her. Jade dropped to her knees, screaming a cry she'd never howled before. The need to swallow her bottle of pills that were supposed to "help" only became much clearer while she stared at her dead cat. Jade pounded her fists against the stairs as hard as she could.

Only a fucked-up moron would accidentally kill their cat! Ready to start blaming Timothy instead of herself, Jade turned around and sat on the step, screaming more. She picked the shards of skull from the bottom of her foot, deciding she would kill herself at this point. Now, more than one living being had been negatively affected because of Jade's existence and actions, there was just no point in living anymore. Especially with the guilt.

"Jade, dear." Tim flipped on the light from the dining room, holding Baxter who was alive and well.

Baxter's tail flapped back and forth slowly against Tim's muscular forearm. The dining room—to the side of the staircase and the front door of the house—lit up a portion of the first floor of their home.

Jade removed her hands from her face. The tears were still fresh on her cheeks, but she was able to clear them and double-check the stairs behind her, as well as the bottoms of her feet. No dead cat.

She walked down the last few steps and hugged both her husband and Baxter. The cat eventually wriggled out of the embrace, but Tim reciprocated the squeeze. He then opened the front door. The light on the front porch showed the normal nightlife to Jade—literally nothing there. Just their front porch.

Tim and Jade walked into the living room. Though the TV reflected objects moving behind them, Jade ignored the black mirror. The reflections were just showing Tim and Jade moving about the kitchen. Baxter showed up again, jumping onto the couch and preparing to lick himself. He watched his silly owners walk room to room, doing whatever they were doing.

"Okay, woman. That is the whole house. It's just the three of us. We can go back to sleep now, yes?"

"Yes," Jade confidently answered, but she focused on the reflections of the TV.

They both started back up the stairs yet images still moved within the turned-off electronic.

There's no one there. What is it reflecting? What are they trying to show me? Jade shook her head hard to rid her mind of thoughts that made no sense. She followed Tim up the stairs and looked back at Baxter with an apologetic stare.

"Love you, Bubba!"

Baxter watched Jade go up the stairs and relaxed into a ball of sleep.

The couple walked back into their bedroom, and Jade let out a sigh of relief. She finally felt "normal." Her heart wasn't pounding, her mouth was salivated, and a cool calmness had taken over. She was tired. Jade looked over at Tim, about to apologize for the millionth time, but he interrupted her thoughts.

"Look, dear. I'm sorry. But this had to be done. And if it has to be done, then we'll do it every night so I can assure you that you're safe with me. Okay?"

Jade thought about what her husband had just proposed. She didn't like it. Jade didn't want to experience what she'd always experienced over and over and over again. She wanted to get better, wanted her husband and their cherished cat to be unaffected by her own flaws. So, she compromised.

"Timothy, we didn't look at the terrace." Jade turned her head and pointed toward the doors to the left of their bed, which opened toward the beautiful second-floor patio. She figured there could be nothing—or no one—there. But the reassurance she always needed could be the next step to the recovery of her mental health.

Tim agreed, placing his hand on her shoulder. He then walked over to the long curtains covering the glass doors, flicked on the light switch from the inside, and opened the terrace doors. A small gust of wind blew the curtains, like ghosts flapping elegantly, a dance with gravity. Jade stood up and saw Tim on the porch. He smiled at her, and she smiled back. Their beautiful home, normal, untouched, and only haunted by her thoughts.

There is literally nothing wrong, Jade thought.

Tim walked back in and locked the doors behind him.

Jade crawled into bed, pulling the covers tight and embracing the warmth her body provided. Tim went through the house, turning all the lights back off. Though Jade felt a pang of paranoia, Tim inched back into bed with her, warming her further with his embrace. She felt safe again. Her heart rate slowed and she started to fall into a deep sleep, clasping his hands against her breasts.

The man Jade had seen earlier emerged from beneath the bed and slashed both their throats within seconds.

He stood above them while the couple shook, making gulping sounds. They each took their last breath. He then ran toward their home office, taking the stash of money he had originally been looking for, hidden in the library of books.

The man peeked out of the office and snuck down the stairs. He whispered to Baxter, "You all should have listened to her."

The front door closed behind him when he exited, making the rest of the house's inside truly black.

Dark Places

C HAPTER 3

Saranac Lake, NY
June 2019

"Who cares what they're saying on the news. It's probably bullshit anyway!"

Alexandra figured Ethan was probably right, but it was strange all these places were losing power. Luckily, theirs was just fine.

"You know. You should probably just take those pants off."

Alexandra rolled her eyes at his suggestion then laughed when he chased her trying to grab her ass.

It had been ten years, and they both couldn't feel any luckier they had found each other. She bent over to tease him, then ran to the bedroom, almost forgetting for a minute it was just the beginning of summer. Because of this, the sweat caused her shorts to reach further up into her ass, which just made him even crazier.

Alexandra pulled them down to release the tension. Though she had always been self-conscious with her short, petite build, Ethan had never shown disappointment, even being a foot and a half taller than her.

"Oh my gahhd, you're in the bathroom now? You chased my ass just to get to the toilet!"

She continued to laugh at him while he coughed, peed, and then mumbled about how much of an asshole she was. Alexandra rolled onto her side, pajamas and shorts half way down her legs. She started to wonder what they were actually saying on TV.

Since they moved to the lake, it had been difficult to get a satellite signal on occasion, even for today's standards. They had waved bye-bye to cable a long time ago, which was fine. Fine because the general public was a nuisance and because mainstream media was a joke. However, it was nice to occasionally know what was going on in the world.

Ethan peaked out of the bathroom into the bedroom, flexing his arms and poking out his belly. "Ya like that?"

"You're such an ass."

He then proceeded to thrust his hips back and forth, stripping off his T-shirt and throwing it in her face, like he was some sort of professional. She threw the shirt back at him.

"Flex your Dad-bod to me, sweet cheeks!!!"

She rolled over exposing naked lower body and he dove forward, giving her bum a nice, big smack.

"You're the ass now!" she shrieked.

"I'm an ass. You're a tease. We're even! Want another beer?"

"Nah. I'm tired."

The TV screen finally focused back to a picture of two typical news anchors interviewing another one "in the field" with downed power lines in the background.

"Lex, are you going to the store tomorrow?" Ethan yelled from the kitchen.

"The crews are working now on restoring power for residents in the Saranac Lake area. They are also gathering to prepare for surrounding

areas as reports are coming in on more power loss. When I asked the foreman as to what the situation was, as far as the reasoning behind lines going down since there are no heavy winds and the skies are clear, he said, and I quote: 'No idea, I'm just here to fix it.' Now, Karen and Jim, as you can see..."

"Lex!"

"Jesus, woman, what?" Alexandra yelled in her infamous sarcastic tone.

Ethan came back into the bedroom with some water wanting to repeat his question, but he realized he was tired too. "Never you mind, devil woman!" He snatched the remote from her, turning off the TV.

There was no argument from Alexandra, even though she wanted to know what was happening. She would rather snuggle up with Ethan and pass out. Which eventually, they both did.

Alexandra was in a deep, dreamless sleep. She involuntarily reached her left arm tighter around Ethan, who was half asleep, and moved his body closer to hers. When Ethan entered R.E.M., a violent crash awoke them.

The couple thought it was an earthquake. The walls around them stuttered and shook. Then, when the rumbling dissipated, Alexandra and Ethan attempted to gain their consciousness and composure.

The ceiling above started to tremor. It cracked and creaked so loudly, both were frozen from fear and drowsiness, all at the same time.

The dormer roof above them crashed through the bedroom, encasing the couple inside the triangle of wooden beams and insulation. Alexandra had jumped on top of Ethan just in time, nearly missing being pierced in half by wood, shingles, and other broken materials.

The roof had come down with such force, it punctured the through mattress, anchoring the entire bed in place.

Ethan wrapped his arms around Alexandra as tightly as he could, wondering if this was the moment he was going to die. Alexandra buried her face into Ethan's shoulder and cried. His heart beat against her own chest and she couldn't decide whose heart was going faster.

The walls around them continued to shake, and it sound like thunder. The couple gripped each other inside the deafening chaos. All they could do was lie there, stuck, and listen to what was going on around them. Any intact part of the bedroom ceiling that had survived the roof falling through slowly broke apart and crumbled to what was left of the floor.

The walls suddenly stopped bellowing, and all Ethan and Alexandra could hear were pieces of the house caving in. Trapped in the enclosure, they could only listen, surrounded in pitch-black, no light from the starry night sky getting in.

"*Shit*, Ethan, what do we do?"

Ethan's neck was soaked with his wife's tears and their sweat. He had been in closed quarters like this before, when he was an active marine. Not letting his thoughts go there, he took a couple of deep breaths and thought over his answer to Alexandra's question. The last thing they needed to do was start panicking and not have any strength or logic to get out of this mess.

"*Ethan!*"

"Lex. Please. I'm thinking."

Alexandra gripped him tighter, trying to breathe slowly and deeply with Ethan to calm down. Ethan closed his eyes, then opened them wide, hoping to adjust to the surroundings and figure out the next move.

"Can you roll off of me at all? I want to try and move this fuckin thing."

Alexandra was able to do a half-roll, still on top of Ethan.

"I may be able to scooch down a little so you can lift your arms."

"Do it." Ethan was assertive and serious when he needed to be.

Alexandra obeyed, bent her body upward, as much as the space allowed, and pulled the bottom part of her body backward. This was one of the few times her lack of height actually benefitted her.

Ethan reached up—only about a forearm's length between him and the roof section. He used his abs to lean as much as he could, feeling if he had any more room to lift or punch. Ethan was able to touch the highest point of the angle, and with all his might, he attempted to raise it. Unsuccessful, he huffed and puffed, tried one more time, wailing in pain when his strength was no good. There was hardly any room for him to turn on his side, so he instructed Alexandra to try and feel if there was something they could start picking apart to climb out of the structure.

"It's all fucking solid wood!" Alexandra screamed her frustrations, poking her feet above them and reaching all over the sides with her short arms. She used her fingers and toes to grasp for anything to get them the hell out of there. The more frustrated she became, the more she began to hyperventilate.

"Okay," Ethan said calmly. "Stop. Let's take a breath. We're going to get out of this."

Alexandra relaxed her body and pulled herself back up to Ethan's shoulder. Whether she rolled to left or right, she was still on top of him.

"Well..." Alexandra said, with alarming hesitance in her voice. "Not to add to the major fucking problem we are in. But I have to pee."

"Just go. There's no other choice."

They held each other in silence for a couple of minutes. It felt like hours, but Alexandra did what she had to do. She rolled over as much as she could, crying and urinating on the love of her life.

"Lex! It's okay! We're gonna figure this out. I just think we need to keep..."

Another loud crash interrupted Ethan.

"What was that?" Alexandra whispered.

They both listened. It was outside, picking away at the rubble of what was left of the beautiful, lake-front house. Parts of the home exploded open, more walls caved in and glass shattered, echoing from the front door all the way through to where Ethan and Alexandra lay together, trapped in fear.

———————————

It slithered from room to room, above and below pieces of broken wood. The being knew people were inside somewhere, knew exactly one of the things *it* was looking for was hurt, hiding, or both. Even though it stood outside the house, about twenty feet above the rubble, its tenacle-like appendages guided through the structure. Its eyes and nose, seething with grit and grime, waited to find what it was looking for.

———————————

Ethan covered Alexandra's mouth when she tried to scream. The crashing and breaking noises came closer, with a loud hiss and wet slither. Ethan held his breath, trying to be as quiet as possible. Alexandra took note and stopped gasping. It went silent for a few seconds, and the couple both exhaled in unison.

"Okay," Ethan whispered, "I don't know what the hell that is, but we need to be ready. Is there any way you can lean down again and try and pull something apart?"

Alexandra nodded, even though Ethan couldn't see it. She scooted the lower half of her body back down again and tried with all her might to break a piece of a two-by-four off. While she slapped and punched and elbowed the part of the roof, Ethan continued to try and lift the structure off of them.

The silence within the house broke again. The oily appendage reached above the door to the bedroom and crashed through, interrupting Ethan and Alexandra's attempt to break free. The tentacle bent upward from the floor to what was left of the ceiling, curling its point and waiting like a wolf for its prey to move.

Alexandra crawled back up to Ethan, holding him tight. They both stopped breathing again, but Alexandra's eyes filled with tears. She shut them, but the hyperventilating kicked in and one sniffle gave away their location.

The being's limb went full force and broke through the roof of their mini-prison, grabbing Alexandra at her ankle, coiling up her leg, whipping her entire body back through the house. Every part of her was hurled and hit on the rubble that was once her home.

She wailed her arms, attempting to reach what was dragging her at top speed. Her wrists and legs continued to hit walls, but the final blow was her head banging against the edge of the front door when she was thrown ten feet into the air, and plopping down onto hard ground near the unpaved driveway.

———————

Alexandra figured she had been knocked unconscious. Her head throbbed and her body ached. Her eyesight was blurry and she tried to regain focus while figuring out how she had gotten outside. Alexandra gripped her ankle, writhing in pain, and felt a sticky substance. Broken and confused, she brought her hand closer to her eyes, trying to register what had happened and what was now happening. She winced in pain, opening her palm and spreading her fingers apart, which revealed a clear, gel-like substance. When she started to focus on it, it was gleaming like a dying glowstick.

Oxalate? She thought.

For a second, Alexandra figured it was just the night sky reflecting on the goo—and her beaten body—she looked up.

Behind her, stood a dark, dripping figure—that to Alexandra looked to be 100 feet tall. It was black and viscous, illuminated in the moonlight and scouring the trees around them. The creature began to growl and slowly leaned down, meeting Alexandra's face its with own. Its multiple sets of eyes were giant, black mirrors reflecting Alexandra's crying face.

She started to urinate a little again, backing her body away with her bruised arms. But its opaque face just slowly followed her. The huge head with indented scars, dark purple veins with permanent glass injectables, lifted its chin to look at her.

It had grabbed the wrong one.

"Noooooo!" Alexandra screamed at the top of her lungs, like she knew what had just happened.

The multiple tenacle-like appendages reached back and lifted itself at top speed, returning into the house, causing the ground around Alexandra to quake. It shoved her body a few feet backward and she hit her head on the driveway, knocking her out cold.

———————————

Ethan was already out of the bed, dazed and confused, screaming for Alexandra. He hopped along the rubble on the floor with his bare feet, knowing he had to grab something to defend himself. None of this was a normal act of Mother Nature.

Ethan tip-toed out of the bedroom, grabbing a rifle from the hallway closet. *Locked and loaded,* he thought.

"Lex?" he whispered, knowing deep down she probably couldn't hear him. He made his way down the hallway, surveying the incredible damage to his house,

The slithering sound occurred again, and it stopped him in his tracks.

"Fuck."

The tentacles grabbed Ethan by both of his feet, knocking him flat on his back. It shook the gun from his hands, making sure to knock his skull on the floor. The creature didn't want a fight from this one, but wanted him alive, so it was more careful this time. It brought Ethan outside.

Perfect. Just another one that we need.

Surprisingly, Ethan started to come to. Just as he was realizing he was at least twenty feet in the air, the many tentacles squeezed Ethan's body slightly. He passed out, then shot through the air up to the being's vessel.

———————

A few hours later, the sun began to rise. Alexandra woke up on the driveway, with a pounding headache and dried blood all over her face. She had thought this had all been a nightmare, but understanding the reality, she looked around.

No firetrucks or ambulances had come to the rescue for what she had thought was a tornado or an earthquake. And no Ethan, either.

She lifted herself from the ground with both her arms, but an immense pain shot from her shoulder. Alexandra could hardly stand and was surprised when she maintained her balance. Her legs were almost unrecognizable, covered in bruises and cuts, continuing to swell from the beating she had taken.

Ethan where the hell are you? She was more afraid than ever. Between whatever she had seen earlier and the possibility of Ethan being dead inside the collapsing house, Alexandra still managed to hobble up to the crumbling structure and look inside.

The rising sun broke through the clouds and gleamed into the glassless windows, revealing a mess Alexandra was especially shocked to see. She stepped through the debris, ignoring her broken body and bare feet.

"*Ethan!*" Alexandra yelled with everything she had left in her. She stopped at the end of the hallway when she saw Ethan's rifle. Alexandra knew in that instant he had obviously tried to do something after she had been grabbed and thrown out of her own house.

Trying to keep her balance, fighting back tears, she toppled through the hallway and into the bedroom. Ethan was gone.

There was no blood, no ripped clothing, no evidence of Ethan, and she started to break down. Alexandra ran out of the bedroom, punching what was left of the walls. She tripped over ripped-up floor tiles, pieces of ceiling, and shards of glass piercing the balls of her feet. Alexandra ignored the pain and her thoughts, stepping back outside and trying to regain her breath.

That is when she heard the sirens in the background.

———————

Ethan awoke and opened his eyes slowly. His eyelids were heavy and his brain and body throbbed with a numbing pain. He lifted his head, his eyes starting to adjust to his surroundings.

Before being able to focus, he realized his hands were tied above his head, his legs stretched out and bound as well. Ethan regained strength in his neck and was able to look up. Naked, strapped, and hanging above dim, pulsating lighting, all he could remember was being stuck with Alexandra in bed. The straps across each of his ankles and wrists connected to a thick, black contraption holding him in place. The mechanism on his back was connected to the wall behind him.

Many of these holding contraptions around the space were empty. There were hundreds of them—all tacked to a wall, which glowed a purple, watery hue. The violet lighting from the walls continuously dimmed in and out but was always lit enough to show he was fucked. Because, when Ethan looked down, he saw even more of the wall hangings below him, at least a couple hundred feet down. There were also a few compartments holding more men imprisoned in the same position he was in.

Ethan moved his midsection back and forth. His arms and legs had been strapped so tight he couldn't move them, but he was able to bend his hands, feeling what was restraining his wrists. The material seemed like leathery vinyl, but when Ethan pushed his fingers into it, it felt muddy, like a thick liquid that went nowhere.

Ethan gave up and just yelled. The louder his screams, the brighter the purple lights pulsated from the walls. Ethan ran out of breath and the little energy he had, went to his ears, as he heard other faint screams across from him, below him. The cries dissipated, as did the slow, purple flashes. Ethan's wrist and ankle restraints became tighter, then mutated at the edge of the cuffs becoming sharp hammerheads.

His body shifted when something below started moving toward him. Sounds of scraping metal eased upward, and multiple tentacle-like obstructions connected to Ethan's genitals, piercing his flesh.

Just before Ethan passed out, he heard the rest of the distant screams, wondering what was being taken from him and if this was how he was actually going to die.

To be continued...

Feeder Creek

Bonnie Baxter unlocked her front door with a determined hand, clutching her divorce papers in the other. She couldn't wait to chug a beer and take a shower to wash the day away.

Bonnie was impatient to have her last name reverted to her maiden name. The one she had been born with. The name before she had met the wretched Ted Baxter. Ted Baxter, the bastard and abuser of women. He hated it when she would call him Ted *Bastard*. It usually made those couple of extra bruises she got from him worth it. Bonnie knew how to press his buttons. They both made it easy for each other. Ted was just typically the more violent one.

Bonnie plopped down on their—her—ugly plaid couch, still gripping the folder full of papers, and let the hardly working air conditioner blow semi-cool air on her face. With everything that had happened in court, at the lawyer's, and in the last few months, she was finally rid of *him*. The small house they had purchased together was finally looking like a home again because there was no more trash being thrown around, no broken furniture, and especially no glass beer bottles strewn about.

When Bonnie drank, she finished her beers and put them in the bin, like a normal, respectable adult was supposed to. Bonnie brought the folder with her like a shield to the refrigerator and grabbed her refreshment, knowing she would have to quit drinking soon. Or at least, take a break from it. At this point, however, she needed to calm her nerves and put the paranoia of Ted showing up on the backburner by way of booze.

She sipped delicately from the can.

"Oh, who am I kidding?" she said out loud, guzzling the can's contents and grabbing another from the fridge.

Bonnie continued to numb her thoughts and feelings. She finally put the folder down and walked out to the front porch. The sky was a beautiful orange, stars just starting to peek beyond the trees in the distance. As hot of a summer as it had been, Bonnie took in the small breeze, the scenery of the sun beginning to set, and the sounds of cicadas buzzing as a distraction from the harsh temperatures.

Even though the papers had been signed, she planned on installing cameras at the end of the driveway and all around the house, just to be on the safe side. Bonnie continued to think about Ted the Bastard and how she wasn't innocent in the whole situation, but she decided to stop her thoughts with one more drink and that cold shower.

The humidity dropped throughout the night, so she opened the windows and sat on the new bed she had bought just for herself. Bonnie scrolled on her phone and sipped at another beer. It was fairly late, and though the frogs and crickets still sang their serenades, Bonnie's heart stopped when she heard a *thump* at the front door. She froze for a few seconds, the beer can at her lips, and continued to try and listen.

The humming of the outside animals and insects kept its steady tune, but Bonnie slowly stood up from the bed and stumbled to the deadbolted, newly reinforced front door. There was no one and nothing. Bonnie peered through the living room windows behind the blackout curtains and confirmed no headlights, no car driving by, and no vehicle parked along the driveway. She decided she was more than just buzzed.

Since she had her lawyer and the local sheriff on speed-dial, Bonnie double-checked all the locks and walked back to the bedroom.

Plus, Ted hadn't been to the house in months, and today was the first time she had seen him since their last encounter. Bonnie closed the bedroom window. The sounds of crickets seemed to increase their volume, but she ignored it, got into bed and researched on her phone a dog she could consider adopting.

The next few days were mostly uneventful. Since the settlement, Bonnie had been awarded half for the house, and that money would finance her drinking habits, allowing her time to start looking for a new job. She sat with the ten-year-old desktop on Ted's crummy, little desk, only being able to browse for jobs a few minutes at a time. Though this room had been cleaned, she stared at the holes in the walls they had both punched, cigarette burns in the carpet, and other various stains consisting of brown liquor and blood.

Fuck this. Bonnie continued dredging up old memories, walked away from the computer and closing the office window.

"Only an idiot like you would think that color on the walls in here is a good idea!" Ted shoved Bonnie and punched another hole in the wall.

Bonnie shoved Ted back and laughed when his fist became stuck in one of the many holes.

"You bitch!"

"You bitch!" Bonnie mocked Ted so well now, she was surprised he would still get pissed about it.

A loud, almost squeaking noise interrupted Bonnie's reminiscence. She confirmed the window was still closed, and through the clanking sound of the air conditioner, she could still hear a chirping through the walls. Bonnie reached her hand out to one of holes, and the paint chipped. The drywall slightly crumbled against her palm, and the chirping sounded louder.

"Aw, it's a damn cricket!" *Right?*

The noise became louder and louder, like a siren echoing throughout the entire room. Ted's double-edged ax was leaning up against the corner, and Bonnie thought about using it to add more destruction to the room walls. But the noise dissipated.

Bonnie grabbed the ax anyway, deciding she would try again tomorrow with the job search. She thought about having a beer. It was almost four o'clock, which meant it was basically five. The ax slowed her pace to the fridge, but another *thump!* coming from the front porch froze her in her tracks.

It's Ted fucking with me. What else would it be? Bonnie gained confidence with the ax in her hand, marched right to front door and opened it with a sober authority she had never known she had.

Relieved and disappointed at the same time, Bonne saw no one. The front yard, driveway, and all areas around the house were clear. She ignored the déjà vu and quickly ran back inside, placing the ax next to the door. The loud chirping began humming its tune again, this time from beneath Bonnie's feet. The racket seemed to follow her from under the floor with each footstep, slowly driving her mad. She grabbed two beers to double-fist and ran to her bedroom.

Bonnie assumed the crickets were starting early today, but the sound was deafening. She ran throughout the house, making sure all the windows and doors were closed to try and at least muffle the sound. Bonnie grabbed the ax and went back into the office to pin-point where exactly the chirping had been coming from. First it was the floor in the living room, the ceiling in the bedroom, and now in the office. It was echoing all around her.

"Just make it fucking stop!" Bonnie yelled at the top of her lungs, hardly hearing her own voice.

Tears streamed down her red cheeks when she picked up the ax and started on the walls, bashing in more holes. Which wasn't hard to do, due to the shoddy drywall. After the tenth and final swing of the ax, the chirping quieted down and finally stopped.

She gripped Ted's—her—ax tightly with both hands and rested it tensely on her lap. Now exhausted, she debated if she had really heard anything at all. Bonnie waited for the ringing in her ears to stop and her heart rate to drop to a normal beat before she slowly stood up.

Night fell while Bonnie stood in the corner, questioning her sanity. *It's hot as hell in here*! Between the workout she had just given herself and all the windows being closed...She figured the air conditioner was on its last leg.

The walls of the house had seen every type of physical violence two people could do to each other, except murder. Bonnie had always assumed either she or Ted would die in this place. Their treatment of each other had made it inevitable. They had driven each other mad from the very beginning, and at times, Bonnie wondered why he didn't just kill her. Or why she hadn't suffocated him in his sleep.

The beer buzz was beginning to wear off, and when she turned on every single light in the house, she was sure as shit she heard a vehicle idling in the driveway. She slowly went toward the front door, ax still in tow.

Knock, knock!

Bonnie became enraged. The fear left her mind and body. All she could think about now was burying the ax into Ted the Bastard's chest as soon as she opened the door. Between the strange noises and whatever had just transpired a few minutes ago, she was finally going to give him what he deserved. More than a divorce, more than taking the house and his shitty shit—a bloody death from her hands. She pictured digging a hole to bury him in, probably in the farthest corner of the backyard, then unlocked the fifty locks, ready to swing.

"Bonnie, babe!"

"Jesus. Betty, you scared the shit out of me!" Betty's hands were full—one with a twelve pack and the other holding a handle of Feeder Creek Rum.

"Well, since you can't text your best friend back after getting rid of Ted the Bastard, I figured I'd come down here and help you celebrate!"

Betty ignored Bonnie holding the ax and pushed her way through the front door. Her voice trailed throughout the house, and Bonnie just stared down the driveway, trying to focus on the road. The chirping sound started to come back, just as the ringing in her ears had finally stopped.

"Betts, do you hear that?" Bonnie questioned with major concern, closing the door and placing the ax back in its spot.

"What I *don't* hear is you opening us up some of these bottles and pouring us a couple shooters of...Oh wow! Did you vacuum? The place looks almost...clean. And Ted-free!"

"I only got plastic cups fer now. Ted took the glassware, since they were his mum's and all."

"Hey, whatever works! So, whore, how ya been?"

As much as Bonnie had not wanted to be around anyone—not that she really had too many people in her life—she was relieved Betty was there. The more they drank and reminisced, the more the sound became prominent through different parts of the house. Bonnie once again figured she was going crazy because Betty seemed to not hear it. She let the cheap rum, which tasted like asshole kick in, and turned the music up. They drank more, reminisced more. Finally starting to feed good, Bonnie filled Betty in on the last few months of her life.

"Bonnie, babe, he could have fucking killed you. I'm so glad you got out when you did. I wish I could have helped more." Betty poured more liquor into each of their cups. "Remember that time when you had the few of us over and all Ted did was sit in his office with the door closed? Only coming out to get a beer every five seconds? He was pissed we were all getting too loud and gave you that fucking black eye? If only I hadn't missed when I threw that vase at him…"

"I may have got the black eye, but you were the cause of the fifteen stitches to his temple!"

"What was he always doing in there? Rhonda and Terry were always freaked out. They stopped hanging out here after that night, ya know. Terry was so scared of my left hook, he left me a few weeks later. Rhonda just stopped callin'."

"Yeah," Bonnie said solemnly. "She stopped calling me too."

"Heard she's engaged now."

"Well, that mullet and big ass was bound to reel in one of the hicks in the damn town!" Bonnie laughed at herself and Betty giggled even harder.

Thump!

"What the hell was that?"

Betty continued to ask louder, but after the second, amplified thump, Bonnie turned the music down. All she could hear was the chirping beneath her feet. The chirps synchronized with each footstep of Bonnie's, like a sick, infested symphony just waiting for Bonnie to crack.

"Betts, I've been hearing this shit all night."

"No, I mean on the front porch, ya idiot." Betty's insults contin-ued. She went to open the front door, seemingly pleased to see there was no one around. She slammed the door and watched Bonnie grab the ax and stumble to the office.

"Betts, I've been hearing this on and off for the last few days. I know it's in here."

"Bonnie, I hear it too. Figured it was just the acres of wildlife you have out back."

The screeching suddenly became so intense, Bonnie dropped the ax and both women cupped their hands to sides of their heads. Betty dropped to her knees and tried to scream, but the blood coming from her ears distracted her. Bonnie remained focused, crawling to one of the holes in the wall she had made earlier. The piercing shrill echoed throughout the house, but Bonnie ignored her own bleeding ears and reached through the hole. She grabbed what felt like a battery. It was cold, metal...but had moving parts.

The noise stopped.

Betty gasped for air. She sobbed, looking at the blood on her hands that had come from her ears. "Bon..."

"*That bastard*!" Bonnie became enraged again. She knew now what had been happening.

It was Ted. Ted the Bastard trying to get his last trick in. She opened her hand to show Betty what had been in the wall.

"Is that what he was doing all those times?" Betty questioned, wiping away the tears, snot, and blood from her face.

Bonnie had revealed a mechanical insect resembling a cricket. It even had small metal antennae and what looked like a miniature speaker in between two bronze wings. It buzzed and twitched in her palm. As soon as the sound began again, she threw it on the floor, stomping on it with all her might. The tattered old lady slippers she was wearing didn't have enough force.

"Bonnie, babe, the fucking ax!"

"Right." Bonnie complied with Betty's suggestion and smashed the metal cricket with all she had. She pictured Ted's face and kept going. Bonnie remembered all the trips to the hospital, the broken nose, and the black eyes. The insults, the fighting, the decrease in value to their—*her*—house encapsulated her, and all she saw was red.

"Bonnie. Bonnie!"

Not only was...whatever that thing was...dead and broken, so was the carpet and part of the flooring. Betty stared at Bonnie's hands gripping the ax's wooden handle. She walked over to her friend, but Bonnie just dropped to the floor, defeated. Bonnie screamed and cried for what felt like an eternity, rocking back and forth on her knees, still holding the ax. Betty hugged her friend as tight as she could, and just when she was about to suggest another shot of Feeder Creek there was another *thump* at the front door.

They turned their heads in unison, wondering what, if anything, was next, aside from their sobriety.

"Okay, pull yourself together. We've got each other, woman. That Ted fucker is gone and may have had the last laugh, but he'll never know it...right?"

Bonnie went to grab the bottle of liquor then opened the front door to check on the noise.

"Wait, Betts..."

There was Ted the Bastard standing on the front porch, holding a remote control in one hand and a machete in the other. He slashed through Betty's torso all the way up to her throat. Blood sprayed from her body and rained on the vacuumed carpet and newly washed curtains. She managed to hold on to the bottle, dropping into darkness without it breaking.

Bonnie then snapped out of her sadness and back into her rage. Betty was limp, bleeding out, lying in between Bonnie and Ted, her blood creating a path guiding Ted to scared, little Bonnie.

He managed to see behind Bonnie into *his* office. The broken creation that had taken months to perfect. Ted lunged forward, throwing the remote at her head. It was an old, heavy thing he had re-wired from a toy car he had had for years. The corner of it just grazed Bonnie's temple.

Still holding the ax, she watched Ted the Bastard come at her with the machete covered in Betty's blood.

Slow to get up, Bonnie pictured the hole in the backyard she had imagined previously. Digging it deeper and deeper and kicking Ted's useless body into it. The daydreaming almost got the best of her. Bonnie fell forward, swinging the ax behind her in Ted's direction.

"*You bitch!*" The ax only nicked Ted in the arm, slowing him down for just a few seconds.

"*You bitch!*" Bonnie once again mocked him, then crawled toward the bottle in Betty's hand.

The hand was still warm. Bonnie pried the bottle from Betty's fingers, ignoring the fact that her best friend was dead. Betty's blood seeped into Bonnie's clothes.

"Oh, Bonnie. You weak, pathetic cunt. You will *never* take anything from me again."

Ted started to crawl on top of her. The weight of his body pressed her mid-section to the floor, shooting pain from her tailbone, through her spine, to her neck.

"Oh, Ted. Don't you know what's next?"

Bonnie hit him on the side of his head with the bottle of Feeder Creek so hard, not only did the bottle shatter, but Ted the Bastard started to seize. She managed to kick him off her. Saliva bubbled and foamed out of his mouth. Bonnie stood up with one foot on his chest, gazing upon him with a sick desire while he suffered and continued to twitch.

She ended it all with one thrust to his chest with his own machete.

Bonnie then sat in puddles of blood, contemplating what to do next. The late-night summer sounds sang a peaceful tune. Bonnie looked at the two bodies in her living room and decided to dig two separate graves. She figured Betty would understand.

Hours later, Bonnie watched the sun rising through her kitchen window while she washed the blood and dirt from her hands. Sore and still kind of drunk, she processed what had happened and what story she could concoct if anyone ever asked about Ted. Or Betty.

Bonnie figured she should just try and sleep at this point, since exhaustion was setting in. She crawled into her bed, feeling regret, then feeling nothing.

Bonnie drifted into sleep, but a noise alerted her wide awake.

Chirp, chirp!

Wink

"**W**HAT THE FUCK, MARK? YOU FUCKING KILLED HER! THAT'S YOUR FUCKING WIFE!!!"

The makeshift lighting flickered perfectly—slinging back and forth, light on Marie's dead face, then the light on the back of Mark's scratched neck. Back and forth. Back and forth. The lights continued to sway violently, because, during the struggle, fists and heads hit them. More than once.

The brawl lasted a minute. Maybe two. It's funny how, in the moment, time seems to last longer. Chris just sat there with a blank stare. Shock? It's hard to tell with him. Sarah was hiding in the corner with her knees as close to her face as she could get them. David ran to her, clueless how to comfort her, but all he could do was stop yelling at Mark, hold the love of his life, and think.

How the hell were they going to get out of this one?

————————

The night Sarah met David was fate, a blessing—whatever you want to call it—but she was finally at the right place at the right time, even though it didn't seem like it at first. She was on the billionth date with the billionth guy, just trying to start something real and adult. Aside from there being many jackasses out there, her independence and intelligence seemed to scare off most men. So did her honesty. But what scared her this time was this blind date.

She wasn't an idiot, always having knives on her. Easily accessible defense keychains, spray mace, and fun little tactical pens in every pocket of her purse. But this guy...seemed already drunk when she first met him at the pub and proved he was nothing like he had been while they conversed online and via texting.

After the first twenty minutes, Sarah was planning her exit strategy. She wanted to be as un-dramatic as possible, because she never knew how some asshole was going to react to rejection.

"All right, baby. I'm gonna piss! Then we should dance! I know you love this 80's shit!" He yelled with an annoying slur in his voice.

"Yeah, actually..." Before Sarah could finish her sentence, the date stumbled away. She started to finish her drink, when she noticed a group of men on the other side of the room celebrating something.

They were a little rowdy, but seemed happy. Sarah took large, controlled sips from her drink, and cheers'd to herself for yet another dating failure. One of the men in the rambunctious group looked at her. She made eye contact him, and he winked. Sarah wanted to roll her eyes, but this felt different. So, she just smiled at him. Then, crazy-drunk-date guy came stumbling back, snapping his fingers and still slurring his words about some song he had paid to play just for her.

"Ya know...I think I'm all set. I'm just going to go home," she said, her tone not exactly polite-sounding.

His eyes seemed to get darker, and he stopped drunk dancing.

"No, baby. I bought you a drink. You owe me a dance, plus some."

Sarah was obviously uncomfortable. David being the good guy he is, decided he should step in. Liquid courage or not. But before he could, Sarah pushed the guy off her.

Not bad, David thought. But the guy tried grabbing her again, so David finally intervened.

"Heyyy girl! Thought that was you! How ya been?" David moved his way in between them. He gazed directly into her green eyes, winked again, and then looked at the douche bag. "And you...Aren't you leaving? Bouncer has something waiting for you at the door." One hand clenched and the other patted the drunkard's chest in a friendly yet condescending way.

Drunk-date guy at first wanted to size David up, looking at him up and down, puffing his chest out, standing tall. He then chugged his beer with a sigh and walked away. "Fuck you, whore!"

"Jesus, what the hell was I thinking?" Sarah said, looking at David. She was able to hide her embarrassment—and her gratitude—quite well.

"Hey, I've been there. Females are just as crazy." David noticed Sarah clutching her key chain. "Hey check it out. We have the same flashlight." It was one of those "tactical" ones people could purchase from typically shady survival websites.

"Hah...No shit..." She was intrigued but still guarded.

"Hey, David! You done being a hero or you gonna take some shot with us?" The men David had been celebrating with kept yelling while he attempted to continue the conversation with Sarah.

"So, my friend Mark is getting married tomorrow. And well...there's shots. Would you like to join us? I'm David, by the way."

Sarah looked into his eyes. "Fuck it!" She chugged the rest of her drink. "I'm Sarah." Then joined David and his friends.

———————

When everything happened, the couple knew they weren't completely prepared. Most of "prepping" for them was a hobby. There were always discussions about how much food to buy, grow, and store. Which weapons to purchase and how much more ammo could they stock pile...At times they didn't take it seriously.

They had their bug-out bags, first-aid supplies, water purifiers, mapped-out getaway routes, two-way radios, batteries, and camping gear. Even an SUV specifically for getting away if and when a time called for it. The biggest problem was shelter. If they had to stay put, there was no basement, no bomb shelter. There was no quick alternative to protect them from what was about to happen. Luckily, there were Mark and Marie. Along with their bat shit crazy friend, Chris.

In the very beginning, the news stations seemed to over exaggerate. When Sarah became scared, it was beyond paranoia.

"Are we under-reacting?"

David shrugged at her question. He stayed cool, calm, and collected. But when the Earth started rumbling and the news stations started blacking out, both Sarah and David knew they were going to have to pack up and drive their asses to Mark and Marie's. Stat.

Sarah had been introduced to Mark and Chris when she met David at that pub. They didn't bother her at first. All three men seemed fairly normal. Normal for her standards. They all had a similar mind-set—prepared, no bullshit, ready to fight, ready to survive. But fast-forward a couple of years later, with many gatherings, parties, and barbeques, Chris and Mark would make statements that were odd. These statements were made when Marie was in the other room or on the other side of the yard.

"I'd fuck her if she was dead, she's that hot!" Or "What do you think zombie pussy actually smells like?"

Sarah laughed most of it off, figuring they were just harmless idiots. She also had no problem telling them so. Mark and Chris knew Sarah was "one of the guys," and she wouldn't have been accepted into their circle had it not been for David. Both men were secretly jealous—and disgusted—their friend had met his perfect match. This jealously would sneak out with passive aggressive remarks.

Mark had Marie because Marie was cute, small, and subservient. Chris had no one because he was an asshole and lived vicariously through his friends. Mark and Chris had been friends for years, and Marie had been welcomed into this odd triangle because she was truly in love with Mark. Also, Marie had no problem learning, at an amateur level, about knives and guns. She liked them. And Mark liked them. So, he liked her. So, they got married.

Chris had been the best man in their wedding. Eventually, the three pooled their money together to build an underground bunker. One that was extravagant, state-of-the-art—the kind seen in TV shows written about by true survivalists.

David was all about this life and supported his friends. When he and Sarah got serious, he showed her the bunker. She was excited and felt safe about the future, in case anything catastrophic were to happen.

But then it did.

"We have to get the fuck out of here. *And now.*"

Sarah blocked David's voice out of her mind, but she knew he was right.

David was very calm driving to Mark and Marie's bunker. His seriousness persisted during the short drive, but Sarah struggled to hide her panic. The world was literally ending. At least, the human race was. She hoped she had remembered to grab everything, like they had always practiced. Though she was relieved they had a place to shelter when there was no place to go, her guts felt like they were starting to ball up. That pit that forms in your stomach when you truly feel like something just might be an awful fucking idea. That moment when your palms begin to sweat and your eyes twitch.

Sarah was not necessarily worried about death because that was inevitable. Whether it be sooner or later, death wasn't the issue. It was *how*. And *when*. She looked at David and grabbed his arm while he switched gears. He was so good at being the more logical one of them both.

"Are we even going to make it?" she asked him.

"Well..."

They were minutes away from the spot. The sky opened and turned bright orange. They both stared upward—the sky, the road, the sky, the road. David appeared to be afraid, something Sarah had never seen throughout their entire relationship.

"Look," David said, "I don't know what's going to happen. But I do know one thing. I trust you; I trust you with my life. More than the idiots we're about to 'bunk' with."

"Why? Because they're crazy?" Sarah laughed. But then she realized David wasn't exactly kidding either.

"I'm keeping a revolver in my boot. You are the only one who knows about it. I don't plan on taking my boots off anytime soon, not in front of anyone. You understand?" David went on to explain there were only six shots and none of the shots are meant for either himself or Sarah.

They were going somewhere with three other people. Six shots. Three other people. Six shots. Three other people.

Just when Sarah was about to vocalize her understanding, the sky grew brighter, blinding, then blackness painted the sky. The fucking car died. Along with their cell phones and everything battery-operated they had on them. It would have been absolutely pitch-black, but the sky was crackling bright. And then the shadows…

"*Shit*!" David grabbed some matches out of his pants side pocket. They were less than a quarter of a mile away from Mark and Marie's. "Grab what you can and get ready to fucking run."

The path to Mark and Marie's looked further away than it really was. Sarah kept up with David as best she could with the backpack weighing her down. They were lucky the sky lit their way. She ran peering up, then glanced at David's back. Everything above them appeared to be on fire. The shadows painting the orange sky made everything terrifying. It was like some sort of fucking nightmare. Everything was getting brighter and darker at the same time. But the faster Sarah ran behind David, the closer they were getting.

"Hey douche bags!" Of course it was Mark yelling, with Chris holding some sort of torch behind him.

"Yo!!!" David grabbed Sarah's hand and winked at her for reassurance

They both jumped down to where Mark and Chris were. Marie greeted them with liquor. Everyone had questions, but not one of them had a clue what was actually going on.

"Jesus Christ man, we almost didn't make it. The car died, and we just ran for your place. Everything fucking died. The car, the phones, our batteries…Everything. What the fuck?" David went on to explain how an EMP—or something else—had happened. They were clearly not prepared.

Luckily, Marie was comforting.

"Well…we have booze, food, and power! We'll figure everything else out soon!" Marie handed out shots of liquor and all seemed okay at the time.

And for a little bit of time after that.

"Well, ya shits, this is it. And it's for real," Chris said, sounding pompous. He wasn't wrong, though.

Mark and Marie were already finished loading boxes of MRE's down the hatch. Sarah hid her anxiety because she didn't want to seem weak, but when it's the actual end of the world, how could someone be calm? Calm—like Chris.

It creeped her out. David noticed it too, but he hid his worries much better than Sarah. Then, there was Mark. He was douchey, the jock-type—and almost as arrogant and insecure as Chris.

Marie was busy being the "mom" to the group. She wanted everyone to be as comfortable as they could be, considering the situation. Marie also attempted to hide her anxiety but failed. Her fear came out in spouts—by yelling. Mostly at Mark.

"Fuck, baby, what are we gonna do? How long are we going to be down here? Is this even enough?" Marie continued to whine. She worried about oxygen, or radiation, or electricity. "Water? Food? Toilets?" she yelled, slowly and surely losing her shit.

So were Sarah and David. They just did it silently.

"Just calm the fuck down, babe." Mark was so condescending, it made Sarah want to smack him.

Once they were underground, all Sarah could do was watch Chris in the corner. It was hard to read him because he either looked annoyed or satisfied, or both at the same time.

The first night, the group actually had fun. There seemed to be an endless supply of booze, and the group celebrated the end of civilization.

"Humans are a plague anyway, am I right?" Chris was an idiot. But when he clutched his rifle and bottle of scotch, he seemed less idiotic and more irrational beneath the poor underground lighting.

The scrawny, conspiracy theorist was just trying to explain the end of the world, without knowing what *actually* happened. His opinions and beliefs always trumped facts.

"You know, Chris...Mark and I considered giving you up for adoption. But then we realized we needed your ammo!" Marie said, then laughed. She spoke clearly, regardless of how much liquor she had drunk. Marie was pretty funny too, considering it was the apocalypse and all.

Chris gave her a death stare when she said that. Only Sarah seemed to notice.

When Chris noticed her, he laughed it off and threw Mark the bottle of scotch.

David also drank, just observing, saying nothing...He knew what was concealed in his boot didn't concern anyone but reminded himself silently that it was there.

Then he winked at Sarah.

After a few more nights and drinks, Mark and Marie danced to some Motown song. David started to join in, but Sarah watched Chris get a little closer to the light and music. It had only been a couple of weeks in, but Chris had that same goddamn look on his face.

"So, what are you waiting for?" Sarah handed Chris the bottle.

"What do you mean?"

"Well, this is what y'all wanted, right? What's with the discontent-face?"

Chris took a swig and handed Sarah back the bottle.

"It's only just begun..."

Sarah became bored with the conversation while Chris became creepy and dull. She joined the others to dance. But she was pretty sure she heard Chris say "bitch" at the end of their conversation.

Sarah danced with her friends and thought about how she had never been close with any of her family, especially now the world was ending. David had his relatives all around the area, but they weren't prizes either. Mark, Marie, and Chris had been the next best thing.

However, anything that didn't involve the odd triangle, David had an absolute talent for getting him and Sarah out of it, politely. She remembered a wedding—or maybe a reunion—they had both been at. An aunt or a cousin or whomever, holding a plastic wine glass filled to the rim, came up to Sarah and David at a food table, babbling about marriage, stating, "Nothing is right unless it's under God's house!"

Sarah rolled her eyes, but David respectfully grabbed her by the hips to dance. He winked at her, holding her close this time, pointed at the aunt/cousin/whomever, and whisked Sarah away, once again into the safety of their own togetherness. David hated confrontation. Sarah basked in it. But David could at least do the saving.

———————————

When David brought Sarah to Mark and Marie's bunker for the first time, he had been abnormally excited. Sarah was delighted too, but then became less so when Chris decided to take over the "tour." Chris had been a huge part in not only funding the excavation, but he helped design, create, and innovate everything involving it.

"So, we've already stocked a food supply here. Mark and I have been prepping for years, so when those damn terrorists take over and there's a nuclear war, we'll be good for months. Years, even!" Chris stated smugly.

Sarah had rolled her eyes. Not because she didn't take any of it seriously, but because Chris was talking.

"*There is also power, which we have generated via solar,* including *back-ups with gas generators over there in a ventilated room. Which means if we had to, we can actually survive! Mark even got extra masks, Hazmat suits, ammo…Basically everything you would need! I obviously started stocking up on tampons, because* duh. *They're not going to think of necessities." Marie looked proudly at Mark, almost obsessively.*

He shook his head, then continued to speak over Chris.

"Right here is the emergency hatch—it exits the south end of the woods. Now, we're all only showing you all of this because we trust you both. We're in this together if shit hits the fan. WHEN *shit hits the fan." Mark was serious.*

Sarah and David both took note.

Chris proceeded to explain how everything was powered. He also shared how he "spared no expense" and paid more than the "Swedes" to build additional entrances and exits so no one would ever be fucked in a situation. Mark rolled his eyes.

"It's safe. There are supplies. We'll all be good. As long as this idiot doesn't lose his shit!" Mark gave Chris a "noogie," like adolescents who were proud of their pillow fort.

But this wasn't a pillow fort. This was real deal survivor shit.

David, continuing to be excited, looked at Sarah. She, too, was impressed but also didn't feel like trying to survive with these idiots. The instability of the trio worried her, but she faked her optimism and asked Marie to continue showing her around.

"Look, if anything happens, anything weird or bad, here's where some extra supplies are." Marie took Sarah around to one of the back rooms in a corner.

Sarah wasn't sure if she should take Marie seriously or not. The guys talked more logistics in the background.

"Mark and I are supposed to always be prepared, right? Well, I'm telling you this. And only you. Just in case. In case..."

"Babe! You aren't scaring the newbie, are ya?" Mark yelled from the other room of the bunker. He had a funny way of intuitively knowing someone was going to talk shit about him.

"No, babe! Just showing Sarah the ropes. Duh!" Marie replied, grabbing Sarah's hand and looking her straight in the eyes. She pointed behind a canister of fuel or food, or whatever it was. "This is here. If you need it. And hopefully, you never will.

"Babe!" Again, Mark was annoyingly persistent.

Sarah nodded at Marie, and both women walked back toward the guys.

"You're not the only one allowed to give a tour just because you have a dick, babe." Marie was suddenly her funny and cute self. She walked toward Mark but she looked back at Sarah.

Sarah, unknowingly and oblivious at the time, didn't understand this was another way out.

Marie, knowingly, had predicted what certain types of men were capable of.

Mark realized what he had done as soon as David screamed at him, but he also did not give a shit. His pupils became plate-sized, lips as white and tight as a ghost's. David stepped away from Sarah, toward Marie, just wanting to save her. He always wanted to save everyone.

Before David could even check for a pulse, Mark swung his forearm, smashing him in the jaw. Blood sprayed from David's mouth, his heavy body falling to the concrete floor next to Marie.

David knew he could take a hit, but what he hadn't been sure about was how long he could last if Mark kept going.

Chris pushed Marie's body off to the side, then slowly made his way toward Sarah. A pretend hero, she secretly called him. *A wannabe*. She had called Chris a lot of names, because she had always known that he was human trash.

Still unmoving, Sarah stared at Marie's eyes, now rolled into the back of her head. She knew David was in trouble, measuring his dick with Mark, by way of a fist fight. However, Sarah still couldn't move. She just kept looking at Marie's face. Marie's *dead* face.

Then Chris grabbed Sarah's arm, sliding her ass to the opposite corner of the room. The burn from being dragged across concrete and Chris's grimy hands touching her knocked Sarah out of the shock.

"What the fu..."

Chris knocked Sarah out with the butt of his rifle. He laughed at how easy it was. He continued to laugh, realizing he was surprised how easy it was.

Sarah started to come to, but all she could remember was that asshole hitting her in the face with his gun. She wanted to wipe the tears and dried blood from her face, but the three men were talking, so she stayed as still as she could and listened.

"Look man," Chris said. "We've been down here for a while now. Just let me do it. Watch or don't watch. She's pissed you off for years and now she's dead. We might as well reap the benefits. Don't even try to downplay it in front of David how fucked up you are."

"Mark, what is he talking about? And more importantly, *who* the hell are you? Both of you! How many goddamn years have we known each other, and you wait until *just now*, the end of *the fucking world*, to show your true colors?" David yelled in between catching his breath.

Mark snickered while Chris smirked. "Look bro...You've known us. You've always known us. But you've also been willfully ignorant. You're suddenly distracted by love since Sarah has been in the picture. We've accepted that...and even her. But now this mutual acceptance is going to cost something. Then it will pay for something—our survival. We won't be in here forever. But until then..." Mark's voice trailed off.

Sarah felt like she wanted to vomit. Not just because of the blow to the head, but because everything she had imagined about Chris and Mark was true. She felt even sicker imagining David being just like them. Sarah knew David was different from the other two animals, especially in part by his sanity, IQ, and candidness.

Fuck, have I been wrong about him this entire time? Why did I have to be this blind about David, even during the apocalypse?

Then she remembered Marie was dead. She remembered Mark's eyes before, during, and after he had killed her. She remembered Chris watching like a voyeur. She remembered Chris's grip on his rifle, tightening with every blow to Marie's head and chest. Then she remembered David stepping in...

Mark placed his forefingers on Marie's face, closing her eyelids. He ran his hand down to her neck. She was still warm. Then he was curious and fondled her breasts. Her nipples were peaked.

This is the best time, Mark thought.

"Yo, what the fuck is wrong with you?" David really tried keeping his cool, now aware of what a danger these two dipshits were.

Chris lifted his rifle, aiming at David, then looking at Sarah's "unconscious" body. He grabbed David's throat and pushed him against the wall. David landed inches from Sarah.

Slow to get up, David grabbed one of Sarah's hands and squeezed while Chris was preoccupied watching Mark about to do whatever he was going to do.

Sarah squeezed David's hand back and opened one eye. It was difficult in this situation, because Sarah *knew* the two men could probably kill her in an instant. They had their firearms as the upper-hand—even with David as her back up. But she also didn't want to watch Mark fuck his dead wife's body.

Marie is already dead, Sarah thought. *There's nothing we can do to save her now. Mark and Chris are sick fucks, so it's live or die. And I can only remember where that one exit is in this damn place...*

When Sarah's head met the ground, when he hit her with his rifle, Chris knew she was out. He watched David comically try and reason with Mark while Marie was lying stiff in the corner.

The light slung back and forth. It would be only seconds before David realized what Chris had done to the bitch girlfriend. Chris had never been too sure about David, even though Mark had known him almost as long Mark and Chris had been friends. But he *knew* Mark the *best*, the *most*, and since shit had really hit the fan, they might as well reap the rewards while the world ended. David could either be game for it all—or *be* the game along with his dumbass girlfriend. Sarah would just be another prize for Chris and Mark, just like Marie had been. And now was.

Chris remembered when David and Sarah had first met because he always regretted not distracting David with more shots of liquor. It usually worked. But, for whatever reason, Sarah was different.

Watching Marie carefully for all those years had been exhausting enough, but Sarah? That was a challenge because Chris couldn't read her. He knew Sarah was one of those women who were hard to control, difficult to domesticate. Marie had been the same way, for the most part. But none of it mattered. Women were always a distraction.

Useless. Chris had known the lot of them talked about him behind his back, questioning why he never had a woman of his own—or at least, never had one for that long. If they had just asked him to his face, he'd tell them those girls had never stood in line. He was better than them, *all* of them.

Even when he found a girl who could hold her own, it just meant she was a dumb bitch who never knew how to keep her mouth shut. Sex with any of them was meaningless, if it ever happened, regardless of the fact he could barely get his dick hard for any of them. It had been a lifetime problem. Chris always showed them the door eventually, blaming every issue on them. The few who found the door before he showed them...those women knew. They had known he was just a piece of shit whose misogyny, multiple insecurities, egotism, and obsession with the end of the world was more important than any female—or any relationship in general.

None of it was more important. Not more important than one particular man.

Another man, other than himself, of course.

It was a secret Chris kept like no other. His paranoia had made hiding it even worse when Sarah came around. Marie was so blinded by "love," she never bothered Chris. All the different women who came and went between him, Mark, and David over the years...he had his worries. But all the women, they never lasted, never stuck around, never matched Chris's self-deluded smarts and wit.

He had doubts his secret would be noticed, or eventually be revealed. The one and only time he got nervous was when he had dated Sam. The relationship only lasted a couple of months, but she and Sarah seemed to get close. The girls had hung out a handful of times without the guys, but he always questioned exactly what those bitches talked about.

Chris thought about first starting the bunker with Mark, building it from the ground up, piece by piece. Mark would always say, "Yo, who gives a shit," when it came to women and what they talked about. Chris remembered Mark also saying: "Now bring down the last panel so we can test this out. You better be right about this solar crap, or we'll really be fucked."

The bunker was his and Mark's. When they were down there, that's all it was about. Chris almost felt humiliated talking about some chick when they were both below the world, but when they weren't talking about tactics, he had to hide his feelings for Mark some other way. Which meant talking about whatever girl he wasn't getting it from.

Mark eventually mentioned bringing David into the mix. Chris knew the guy was like another brother to Mark, so Chris wasn't too upset. David had the same mindset and ideals, so he knew not to protest. But Sarah? And Marie? At least one of them would be the thorn in his fucking side at some point. If Mark couldn't eventually take care of them, Chris would watch, then *take over* taking care of it.

Sarah continued to stay still on the ground, watching and listening. *I knew Chris was a sick fuck.* She thought back to his ex-girlfriend, Sam, and how it had been all she ever talked about right before she left him. Sam had vented to Sarah how he was such a misogynistic asshole with a small dick. Good thing Sam got out when she did. However, all things considered, she is probably dead now. The entire *world* was probably dead now.

Though Marie had showed Sarah every inch of this place without Mark and Chris knowing, an exit might not be the best bet at this point. It was hard to be in survival mode when your head was pounding and you were about to watch people you've known for years become necrophiliacs because *they* were the ones who couldn't handle the end of the world. Ironic, in the sick, sense of the imagination. Sarah knew she'd eventually be next, and she'd be damned if she would let that happen. David would die before it would happen. But then what would take after they *both* died?

I'll be damned if any of *that fucking happens,* Sarah thought, trying to plan her next move.

The squeeze she gave back to David's hand reassured him that she was okay. He knew Sarah was at least conscious and aware. He also assumed she could hear and see everything that was going on. David shook off the blow to the head from Chris—it wasn't that hard of a hit.

"What do you mean I've known you for years? I didn't know you being this kind of a sick asshole, Mark! Why even bring us down here?"

"You don't have to play it up in front of your girl. She's asleep anyway. I figured you knew that after my bitch wife, Sarah would be the entertainment for a while. *Haha,* what man?! You think the food and booze and whatever else we have down here is the *only* entertainment? Alive *and* dead, we will have to eventually carry on the human race. You and Chris have my permission to practice on Marie. We'll be down here for *months. Years,* even! Why did I...*we*...bring you down here? It's called an agenda, asshole. And when it clears up out there, we'll have an entire race with the agenda."

Mark's speech chilled David to the bone.

David squeezed Sarah's hand again and slowly got up. He looked at Chris while Mark was ranting about these insane, grandiose plans. Chris's pupils were dilated, focusing on Mark like he was bowing to a god, just without the actual bowing.

Mark appeared even more insane. David had always considered himself a fairly smart guy, but in this situation, who would know what to do?

Sarah knew survival was the only thing on his mind. Obviously. But how the fuck were they going to survive this disgusting situation without being overpowered, killed, and apparently raped by these psychos?

Sarah did not want to depend on David, but she kind of had to at this point.

She knew what is in his boot, too.

Chris constantly glanced back and forth, looking at whatever Mark was doing with Marie's dead body, then keeping watch on David and Sarah. David was waiting for just the right moment, fully hoping Sarah's intuition matched his. They had to depend on each other for whatever was about to come next.

Sarah continued to pretend to be unconscious, and even though her head continued to pound—and bleed—she was mapping out every area of the bunker. She breathed in and thanked Marie silently for showing her the corners. But it was difficult. Her head hurt hard because of that asshole, Chris, and she couldn't think straight. She was still nauseous, now not only because of the blow to her head, but because she could only imagine what was going on in the other room.

David dropped back beside her and started to vomit. A lot. Which also got Chris's attention.

"*Haha*! What's wrong, pussy? You know you always wanted to do this!"

After Mark was done fucking his dead wife's body, he walked out like he was a new man. He spit in the corner, zipped up his pants, eyes dilated even more than before, then nodded to Chris, like he was giving his dog permission to pick up the scraps off the floor. David noticed this, and Sarah opened her eye for a microsecond.

When Chris put down his rifle, David knew this would be his only chance. He squeezed Sarah's hand again, and pushed himself up from the ground.

"Well, shithead. Was it good for you? Because I can only imagine what is going on outside from here. And what is going outside from here will kick your stupid ass compared to what you've been doing down here you perverted piece of fucking shit."

Mark held his hand up for Chris to see from the next room letting him know he's "got this."

Chris continued to move toward to Marie's corpse, unzipping his pants. Sarah tried as much as she could to not move, not vomit, and not say something to get herself killed.

"*Davey*! You know you wanna! Look at this unconscious, hot piece of ass over there. Don't tell me you've never thought about it!" Mark yelled.

David realized he had never known Mark.

He had to play along and think of *something* for him and Sarah to survive. David also had to figure out a way that wouldn't give his plans away to Mark. Knowing Chris would go along with anything Mark did, David knew the perfect thing. But wasn't like he could just get up and tell Sarah.

"Look, man," David whispered to Mark, "Don't you think I *have* been playing around? This soft spot I have for Sarah is just the human part of me. Honestly, dude...I've never liked the way Chris looked at her, so I've kept it all quiet this entire fucking time. But yeah. I've always wanted to do what you just did."

"I knew it!" Chris climaxed when he heard David's proclamation in the next room. But he was quiet about it. He obviously he didn't want anyone else to know he had gotten off because he heard Mark's voice.

"Well buddy, clean yourself up, because we have a newby! And if you think about it...*two newbys! Hah*!" Mark slapped of Chris's back while his pants were still down and stared at Marie—lips blue, eyes rolled back into her skull.

Chris gathered himself, hearing hear Mark and David moving around, whispering, getting things started for Sarah. This was almost like a baptism for David. Though Chris has his doubts, he got hard again just thinking about the end of the world, the end of Sarah, picturing David fucking her dead, stupid bitch body. Chris zipped up his pants, laughing, then spit on Marie. He knew the best was yet to come.

But so did David.

David felt like he wanted to puke after the conversation with Mark. But if he and Sarah were going to survive, they both had to be in sync and make the next move together.

He shifted Sarah across the floor, so she was underneath him. Mark and Chris watched. David concentrated on Sarah's face, the gun in his boot, and he *knew* Sarah's hand was ready for the knife in hers. It was difficult to plan something like this. All eyes were on them.

All David could do was think. *What the fuck am I going to do? We're underground during the end of the world with two of the most degenerate fucktards in existence, and I'm about to pretend-rape my girlfriend? For their enjoyment? Before we kill them?*

Sarah blinked the sweat out of her eyes, trying to wrap her mind around what was happening. She reached her hands toward her forehead and when she was able to focus, panic set in. David was on top of her, Mark standing behind him.

"Aw, *hell no, girl!*" Chris yelled starting to move toward Sarah.

David stopped Chris with his forearm.

"No, dude. We do this my way, or you get *nothing*."

"Alright, bro, *damn!*"

Mark grabbed Chris and pulled him a few feet away. And that space was all David needed.

Sarah started sobbing. She began to wonder how everything had gone to shit, how everything had gone completely wrong in her life.

Then David smacked her face. Hard enough to hurt, hard enough to bring her back to their own reality. Tears poured down her cheeks, and she glanced over to Mark and Chris. All they did was grin and wait.

"Hey!" David grabbed her face and forced her head toward his.

She peered up at him, as slowly began to unbuckle his belt. When she tried to look at Mark and Chris, who were moving toward them, David forced her face back to his.

Then he winked at her.

As soon as David winked, Sarah grabbed the knife from her shoe and threw it over her shoulder, into Chris's dick. He went down fast and hard, then began sobbing like a little girl. Before Mark could even do anything, David swung his body around, grabbed the pistol from his boot, and shot Mark point blank in the abdomen. He meant to aim for the heart, but he was thankful to at least get that one shot into his friend's body.

Sarah slowly stood, and David pulled his pants up with one hand, gun in the other. Mark was down. Chris was down. Unfortunately, both were still alive.

Fear was out the proverbial window. Sarah was filled with anger and all she could see was red. Forgetting about the end of the world, forgetting about the fact she was in an underground bunker...Her focus was on Chris and Chris alone. The fact David shot Mark didn't even register. The fact that David was still going to have to *deal* with Mark didn't even register. Sarah was ready to kill.

The hanging light suspended above the group swung back and forth again, shining on Chris struggling, then back to Sarah. Shining on Chris struggling, then back to Sarah. Her sweat glistened in the dingy, orange glow. Chris tried to stop himself from going into shock by grasping the knife sticking into his groin.

"You bitch. *Hahahahaaaa*, you bitch!" Chris yelled and laughed, though in all reality, he wasn't sure how much time he had left.

Mark had gone down from the gunshot. Chris slowly slid away from Sarah, only his own ego in the way of his survival. It took every ounce of strength he had to just get half an inch away from her while she approached him. Sarah looked ten feet tall. But he wasn't scared. Until he realized his only defense was the six-inch blade stuck in his dick.

"What the fuck, bro?" Mark gasped in shock, coughing up blood. He cornered himself, staring at David and glancing at the light swinging back and forth, like a noose over Sarah and Chris in the background. Then he met eyes with David.

"What the fuck, *bro*?" David said, mocking Mark.

And that just pissed off Mark even more. Though he knew he was screwed at this point, he thought if he could just figure out how to take these guys out, he was pretty sure the stocked infirmary would be his saving grace. Because Mark always knew what to do. *Always.*

"You're one of us, brother. I thought that was the whole point of this." Mark tried to emphasize his point but just coughed up more blood.

"*This?*" David asked, becoming more enraged. "*This?* This freak show? This was supposed to be about *survival.* About *friendship.* And now it's nothing but a shit show and you ending up a *fucking dead asshole.*"

Mark was slipping away, and David felt guilty. This was someone he had known for over twenty years. Then, David pictured Marie's face. And remembered her raped, dead body just a room or two away from where they stood. Where Mark and Chris had wanted Sarah to be.

"So, what's next, *bro*?" Mark asked, choking.

David watched him bleed out. The shadows of Sarah and Chris moved in his peripheral.

"Well...?" Mark started to cough and gag. More blood came out of his mouth and nose, his face unrecognizable, even to David.

What am I going to turn into after I do this? Then for once, David stopped thinking.

He waited for Mark to stop coughing, and they met eyes. Without hesitation David lifted his knee and stomped Mark's face in until there was nothing left.

While he was stomping, all he could picture were Marie's face, Sarah's face, and the world outside that had turned to complete shit. Marie's face. Sarah's face. David felt more and more nauseous with every smash, but he still couldn't stop himself. He ignored the sound of Mark's skull cracking against the bottom of his boot. When the crunch became just a liquidy squish, David fell to the floor.

———

Chris tried to stay focused on everything in the room. Despite Sarah standing above him, the knife in his dick and him probably bleeding to death, the blurry image of watching David kill Mark with his foot—*his fucking foot*—numbed any physical pain he had. He knew what he had to do, and if he had to do it alone now, he would.

As soon as David's foot went through Mark's skull, Chris tore the knife from his groin and pitched it through the air toward David, hoping to him with the blade. Chris began to apply pressure to his wound with one hand, watching Sarah's reaction. He knew he had to move quickly, plus having to do so with one free hand.

Sarah whipped her neck around to find out what happened with David. It was like everything was going on in slow motion. She was sore, sweaty and filled with rage. Sarah felt like giving up too. *The world is ending, right?*

She had gotten Chris good, so she followed her instincts and ran to David. He was still. *Too* still.

Where the fuck is the knife? Where the fuck is the knife? Her anger and the little logic she had left disappeared, and tears filled her eyes. Sarah's trembling hands flew from David's shoulders to his torso. The knife had landed clean in his hip. And deep.

Fuck. She tried turning David onto his side, but exhaustion was setting in. She was shivering and shaking. But when she saw David's eyes alive and awake, she turned his face toward her, knowing what she had to finish.

Until suddenly, Chris put her in a choke hold mid-thought. He was still pretty strong for being officially dick-less.

Once again, Sarah was being dragged on her ass. The burn from the ground became an all too familiar friend. Sarah jabbed her left elbow as hard as she could right into his groin—or the lack thereof. He went down even harder than he had before.

The sharp pain shot from his legs to his lungs and Chris spit blood right into Sarah's face. He wanted to laugh, but his injuries stopped him. Sarah sat down on her knees and stared at him. Chris began to hold himself. How pathetic he must look to her...

David stood, limping behind Sarah with something in his hand.

Fuck, Chris thought. Beads of sweat poured down his face. He knew Mark would save him any minute now.

"Any minute, right, Mark? Mark? Mark!" Chris yelled, grasping his wounds.

Sarah started laughing like a hyena in heat. Chris just watched her and felt that fear he had always felt but didn't hide it this time. David handed her a pistol.

When the fuck did he get a gun? Chris thought.

Sarah took the gun from David and aimed it at Chris's head. He tried to back away, all while leaning to see Mark—faceless and bloody. He looked back at Sarah and David. His upper body dropped back to the ground. Chris began crying, hyperventilating and holding his bleeding body. This was it. He gotten beat by a bitch and her man.

Sarah emphasized aiming at his head again, stepping down on his shoulder, pushing Chris flat to keep him still.

"Any last words? *Bitch*?" Sarah said, her foot becoming heavier on Chris's body.

When Chris started to open his mouth, Sarah swiftly moved the gun and shot him in his groin. Blood sprayed in every direction, but his deafening, high-pitched screams did not affect Sarah and David. They both already knew he was half dead. Chris had been dead the minute he plotted this whole ordeal with Mark.

Sarah crouched down nose to nose with Chris. "What's with the discontent-face?"

She got back up and pulled the trigger again. His body bounced against the ground from the close-range shot. She just stared. So did David. For a full minute they both watched, confirming the kill.

For that entire moment, it was silent. Except for the hanging light making that slight creak. Slinging back and forth. The light on Chris's dead face. The light on Sarah and David. The light on Chris's dead face. The light on Sarah and David.

"Well," David said, dropping to his knees. "Now what?"

Sarah just looked at him. And winked.

Three Eighty-Five

The place wasn't that great. However, compared to the rest of the shit-holes she had looked at, this was a five-star hotel. Being in a rush didn't help either, but the price, which included utilities…She might as well take it. The corporate attire she wore certainly helped when landlords were choosing a tenant, even though the building maintenance man taking her application wouldn't have known his ass from his elbow.

I knew I shouldn't have settled, she thought, filling out the application Mr. Dummy had given her. *There's no time, though. No time.*

Approval was eerily quick. The email from the landlord confirmed her employment and salary. He wanted to meet in a public place for her to drop off the deposit. When he called her, she ignored the desperation in his voice. Mostly because her hopelessness was just as transparent. He didn't even need the deposit with first month's rent. Strange for the city. The man clearly wanted to secure the place so he didn't have to worry about missing out on money later on. She once again ignored this because she would never be homeless. *Ever* again.

The landlord chose the coffee shop. Not too far out of town, but just enough for her to question where she was going. *There is nothing wrong with this*, she kept thinking. *He sounded friendly and flamboyant anyway, but not like a serial killer or anything*. She continued to justify to herself the need to dwell in the city, as well as the ridiculous ease in getting an apartment by the park. *In the city. Not homeless.*

She started sweating when she pulled into the parking lot of the coffee shop. Her heart pounded. She could never trust her instincts because she was always wrong about everything and everyone she has ever met.

"Devil's advocate," she told herself. "Devil's advocate. How fucking ironic..." She waited in her old, green, two-doored coupe. If something seedy were to happen, at least there would be others in the area to see the landlord walk in first and identify the vehicle she had arrived in.

She spotted the man when he entered the establishment. Normal T-shirt, normal cargo shorts, normal man sandals. *Okay. This is it.* She hesitated at first before finally going in and pretending to look around. When they met eyes, he smiled, waving her down.

He mostly went over logistics, sipping an iced beverage—a latte she assumed. "It's a cute little place", the landlord said. "But if you do smoke, please try and do so by the window. The cat is not a problem. Any issues you have, be sure to address them to *Mr. Dummy.*"

The landlord did state the maintenance guy's actual name, but she was in too much of a rush to pay attention or remember. She handed over the deposit, signed the lease, and was ready to get the hell out of there. *So close,* she thought. *So close to officially having a place again, so close to...*

"Oh, and close to the first, drop off September's rent to *Mr. Dummy* at the apartment. He'll be there cleaning and painting."

Fuck. Another check? Another human being to deal with...let alone Mr. Dummy? Christ, she thought. However, she agreed and stated it wasn't a problem. *Must move. Must move. Must move...*

A couple of weeks after the odd meeting with the landlord, she had to show up to the apartment...alone...and meet *Mr. Dummy* to drop off the first month's rent. *Day-light...Sunday...No problem.*

When she arrived, the door to the apartment was unlocked...and open.

"What the hell, but okay..." she said to herself, walking up the stairs.

He greeted her in the empty, resonating apartment, smiling like a redneck who had just nailed a deer in the head with a cheap shotgun, even though he was eight beers in.

"Hi..." *Shit, what is his actual name?* She fumbled for the check, noticing some strange woman in the tiny kitchen, scrubbing the top of the stove.

His slight speech impediment brought her back into focus, but she still felt dizzy and borderline nauseous.

"So, we're just finishing up on a few things here and I can drop off a receipt to you later this week. Did you want to take a look around? Have any questions?"

The strange kitchen woman just kept scrubbing. The smell of bleach was distracting. She told Mr. Dummy she at least wanted some fresh paint in the living room area and the two ceiling tiles replaced since they were discolored. He was agreeable.

As he should have been, considering the dis-coloring was representative of a sewage leak.

———————————

Getting the boxes through the front door and up the stairs was just as easy. *Well, the bathroom is new and the closet is spacious,* she thought, suddenly feeling vertigo. Unsure why balancing her body had suddenly become a problem, she remembered dizziness was only typical when too many shots of vodka were involved.

Christ. It's been, like, years...

Clearly, there were many odd things about the apartment. But she had been in such a hurry, many of those things were overlooked during the initial viewing and while signing the laughable lease.

"Oh, okay. There's different elevation levels from one room to another. Oh, okay, the bedroom is slightly slanted. Oh, okay, the huge walk-in closet may or may not be below the floor sea level, as the rest of the apartment. That's okay, though. There's storage."

Talking to herself aloud was also something new. *Where's the light?*

"The apartment is on the second floor. Is sea level even a thing? It shouldn't be. Because it's a fucking apartment."

Shit. Then she noticed the thermostat. It was encased in a plastic box with a lock screwed to the wall. Though this type of thing could be typical when renting with utilities included, she also noticed a wall *behind* the wall—a sheet of drywall bursting out like a wooden bubble layered on top. There were old, empty screw holes near the plastic box, causing it to loosen from the wall. *What is happening?*

Falling asleep the first night was more than a chore. Mostly because the bed was so un-level. She'd fall asleep on one side of it, then wake up with half of her body on the night-stand while the other half was off the bed, toes to the floor. *Too much vodka last night. That's all it is.* The cat, however, had no problem balancing. He was a professional, regardless of the lack of furniture. Or gravity restraints, apparently. *The bedroom feels like it's sinking in. It is sinking in. But, nah, it is an old building. Totally safe, though. Totally safe.*

There were many things great about living in a city. The culture, the restaurants, the lack of parking. In fact, there were very few or very many great things. Pessimism aside, living by a park that was right outside her apartment window might or might not have been one of these things.

The gorgeous pond homed temporary ducks. The willow trees provided shade to the trash in said pond. And also, the crackheads yelling at 2:00 am. After a long day of bullshit work, all she wanted was a drink. A drink or ten and the petting of her cat. Her cat, however, scratched at his eyeballs that started to look a little juicy. She of course ignored this, because, well…the cat typically just wanted attention.

The park, however, howled with the voices of the homeless and bellowed with the rantings of drunken college kids just trying to find their parents' cars. She listened to the city serenades through the bedroom window, taking in the roof over her head, even if it may cave in on her at any minute. While she poured another drink, she watched her cat, then lost her balance walking back to her bed.

Her thoughts intruded her mind while she inadvertently rolled back and forth across the mattress, attempting to sleep. She became very, *very* itchy.

Why do I itch? Are these hives? I have no idea. Guess I'll leave and have a professional look at them. But when I try to leave, gravity seems to fluctuate. Am I losing my mind? No. But I itch. The air inside is odd tonight.

Regardless of the windows being open, she was pretty sure the park had nothing to do with the stench in the air. *The cat's eye looks worse. Or am I just being paranoid?* The refrigerator started to hum an odd sound. It had already been loud to begin with, but the noise echoed from the kitchen, reverberating throughout the tiny apartment. There was so much going on, she was unable to decipher one thought from the next. Her senses were in overdrive. *Guess that's why the crumbs in the fridge are warm. Jesus Christ…is that domestic violence I hear next door?*

And yes, yes, it was.

It was the first week she had been living in the new apartment and there just happened to be a couple *constantly* fighting right next door, directly on the other side of her bedroom wall. The stomping on the stairs was a preview before the real show started. She didn't even have to put her ear to the wall to listen to them scream at each other for hours on end. Instead, she could just lie in bed and either laugh or turn the TV on full blast.

I'm laying down, I know I am. But why do I feel crooked? I'm on a damn bed. She leaned up, noticing the TV was crooked. So was the TV stand. As many places as she had lived in, she knew how to arrange furniture. She lit a cigarette and lay back down, her body starting to slide from the bed.

I'm drunk, but I'm not that *drunk...or am I? Juicy-eyeball cat is fine and asleep. Even in a shithole, he manages to get comfortable.* The refrigerator was humming even louder, but along with the ragged air conditioner and even cheaper drugs being smoked by the neighbors next door, she hardly noticed. Eventually, she fell asleep.

The cat, however, awoke and watched everything crawl around her. There was nothing he could do about it.

Weeks went on, and day by day, she found another hive. Red, bumpy, and uncomfortable. The hives became more inflamed the more she scratched them. *Is this the way it works?* She thought. Though she's never experienced an allergy in her entire life, this must be it. Forming odd, constellation-like patterns, she figured her sensitive skin was reacting to detergent. To body wash. To something simple and stupid. *The disgusting City Water? It's supposed to be the cleanest in three counties.* She's only been showering in it for years.

Why is it always so dark in here? She moved to the bathroom as her desk lamp only lit up a part of the galaxy on her back. She was no contortionist either. Stepping down or up continued to be a serious issue with the flooring too. Why was the gravity different? Clearly the floor was at a different height, clearly another floor was built upon the original. *Might as well get drunk. Ignore all of this.*

She laughed as she heard the refrigerator running, as if it actually worked. Touching the red, bumps on her skin as if for some sort of reassurance, she walked toward the fridge. Stepping down from the bathroom, stepping up to the so-called living room, then stepping down to the kitchen. *What is happening?* Her thoughts raced while she literally watched her steps. Grabbing the bottle of vodka from the freezer, taking sip after sip, she decided that tomorrow she would hang up some art. Figuring it would all distract from the crooked floors, the ceiling tiles Mr. Dummy never replaced and everything else in the damn apartment, she also figured keeping busy would be best.

Yes, it will be best.

Bringing the bottle with her, stepping up from the kitchen, down to the living room, then down to the bedroom, she watched the cat staring at her almost mockingly from the bed. "What? You don't like this tiny, second floor apartment?"

He continued to stare at her as she fell on the bed. Attempting to put the vodka on the nightstand, she was also trying to listen to even more screaming on the other side of the wall. *It smells weird in here.*

"Whatever dude, let's listen to some music!"

The cat rolled over and fell asleep like he was always able to.

The vodka bottle then slid off the nightstand like a billiard ball on an uneven table. *SHIT.* Rolling across the bedroom, it didn't have much distance to travel, and also because the floor in the bedroom was lower than the door way to the living room. Which meant the bottle did not break. *AHA! GOOD LUCK IS MINE!* Then she realized the bottle is plastic. *Oh yeah.* She drank from the bottle until she passed out.

A few hours later, flashing blue lights and muffled voices coming through the window woke her up. The bottle was once again on the floor and she was once again half on the bed, half hanging off it. Evening herself out, she wanted to listen to what was going on outside. However, echoes of the damn cat scratching the inside of the litter box in the other room drifted throughout the apartment.

"Dude! Shhh!"

She crawled to the window, just able to see through the small opening. A cop was giving a driver a sobriety test. She could hear almost everything they were saying. It was also 4:00 a.m. and the street in between the apartment building and park was basically surround sound.

The driver was comically trying to walk a straight line and the cop observing this, for probably the one thousandth time, told her to stop and proceeded to tell the driver they're under arrest. The driver started crying and yelling

The cat ran in, knocking over the ash tray, startling her. She then became itchy again, scratching every part of her body she could reach.

"Well, that's enough excitement for one night. Should we go to sleep for real this time, bub?"

The lights from the police cruiser snuck through the crack of the blinds and reflected on the cat's eyes – which looked worse. Slimy, even. Crawling back to bed, she kept scratching until she fell asleep.

The cat once again watched it all come alive around the bed and her. He even tried to bat at her face, but she didn't wake up. While it happened, he ran out and slept on the bathroom floor. There was nothing there so he slept comfortable and unscathed.

This time.

There was a perfect spot on the wall for one of her favorite pieces of art to be hung. As she hammered a nail in, she noticed that damn thermostat again. Encased in a funny plastic jail, it controlled the joke of temperature throughout the entire apartment. As she investigated further, she noticed the plastic case was screwed to the wall with normal, metal screws. However, the plastic case looked like it had been screwed in more than once. You could tell, because the plastic casing around the actual thermostat was not only loose, but you could literally see the previous screw holes in the wall itself.

When she pressed on the surface around it, the problem, amongst many, was that the wall wasn't actually the wall. There was a panel wall loosely placed on top of the drywall. The ridiculous plastic casing housing the thermostat was screwed into the panel, but not through the drywall behind the paneling. Needless to say, from her hammering, the plastic case fell from the 30 layers of wall and smashed to the floor.

Instead of calling the landlord or Mr. Dummy...she was now able to control the thermostat.

After a few times of trying to hang the art, she realized there was no point because the observable layer of wall was not even connected to the layer of wall behind it. Though she lost her balance a few times during this ordeal, she managed to notice the discoloration on the ceiling tiles growing into a larger, stain-like puddle. *Is this real life?* However, now that she had control of the temperature, she might as well celebrate with some day drinking.

The cat just stared at her, blinking away his eye-slime. Questioning the condition of her cat, as well as if there was any point in attempting to make this place look at least somewhat habitable, she gave up and went to the liquor store.

———————

Later on, after taking a shower, the strange smell seemed to grow stronger within the apartment. The steam cleared as she stared at herself in the mirror. There were even more red bumps on her forearms, her ankles. She felt them on her lower back going up to her spine. *Guess I'll make that doctor appointment. AND I'm hungry.* As always, she let her thoughts race while her surroundings continued to grow more and more peculiar.

Climbing down from the bathroom, up to the living room then balancing down to the kitchen...

The refrigerator hummed its usual tune. The stove, hardly used, was propped up between the wall and a "counter," with the two-inch-wide sink next to said counter. She stared at the set up and became incredibly sad. Crying, picking up the cat, they both stared out the kitchen window instead of making something to eat.

It was early evening, late Spring and what seemed to be forever, the cat noticed something and jumped out of her arms. She continued to stare out the window for a few more seconds watching the trees starting to come back to life in the park. Her skin started to feel like fire so instead of more scratching, she reached for the bottle in the freezer.

This will help. It always does.

Continuing to space out again, the awful humming of the fridge snapped her out of it.

FUCK. I guess I'll just have something delivered...

———————

Waking up from a slumber, she noticed the TV was more disheveled than normal. It looked more crooked than before, as did the stand itself. Upon further inspection, the TV wasn't just crooked, it was uneven, half of it on the edge of the TV stand. She KNOWS she didn't move it.

Why would the TV continue to move off its stand?

Sliding off the bed and annoyed with the news anchor reporting on the screen at a weird angle, she put the TV back in its original spot. Stepping back, she realized what the problem was. The entire set up was uneven. She purposely caddy-cornered the TV stand because it was the most logical spot for the TV to be in the bedroom, proportioned to the bed. Luckily from the day drinking, the light was still on, so she said fuck it and tried to even the furniture out.

Moving the stand forward, then backward, then side to side. After the mini workout and once it looked level, she stood up and looked at it again. The TV and TV stand were still crooked. The right side of the stand and the TV itself was STILL leaning to the right.

"What the fuck?"

Once again, the cat was staring at her. His eyes shifted from her to the bed, repeatedly. She didn't see it, or them, but he did. Scared, the cat jumped up and out of the bedroom.

Your ass probably smells the shrimp fried rice from earlier!

It was still technically early, so she divulged in some more drinking. It was difficult enough dealing with the ridiculousness of the apartment, but she figured she could handle it—and everything else—with another good buzz, at least.

"Cheers, Bubba!" Taking a swig and raising the bottle toward her cat, she refilled his food dish. Realizing she was hungry too, again, the vertigo or the alcohol buzz or weird smell changed her mind. So, she just stood in the empty "living room" and stared at the ceiling tiles. The cat's teeth crunching on the food echoed within the room.

As she continued to stare at the ceiling, she had the urge to remove the cheap ass ceiling tile and see what the fuck was causing the black-green growth that seemed to have tripled in size since she moved in. She remembered it was a fairly small, however noticeable, spot in the very corner of the ceiling when she dropped off the first month's rent to Mr. Dummy a while ago. But now...now it was taking up most of the tile and half of the one next to it.

Before doing anything, however, the street lights shining in the two living room windows caught her eye. The window closest to the heavily-stained ceiling tile was a little brighter. *Maybe if I actually open one, the place will air out.* She hesitated, then quickly went to open the window.

Something is wrong.

There's no fucking screen. She slammed the window shut, ignoring her nausea and went to the other window. *No fucking screen in this one either!* Completely frustrated, livid, and a little drunk again, she slammed the window shut and plopped on the hard wood floor. Inadvertently sliding a little to the left, she ignored the whacky gravity and decided maybe she should get some actual fresh air.

But not before taking a swig from the bottle. If she could find where she left it.

There was still plenty of Chinese food left in the fridge from the earlier delivery. She almost forgot about the leftovers, but the humming of the refrigerator reminded her as her stomach growled. Grabbing the food and straightening the microwave back to a level position, she threw it in and decided to try and find something to watch on TV.

As she turned up the volume on whatever local news station to drown out the yelling that was going on next door, everything went dark. The fridge stopped humming, the air conditioner wasn't on and she realized *Fuck. No power.* The street lights outside were still on, illuminating the inside of the apartment. Stepping on the cat's tail, tripping UP from the bedroom, stumbling DOWN to the living room, basically leaning toward the windows, she took a peek. Every building had lights on. *Great.*

Unfortunately, she knew what she had to do. She had to call Mr. Dummy.

She was lucky that Mr. Dummy was so polite and accommodating. It seemed like he already knew what the problem was, however his assumptions weren't exactly accurate.

He lived nearby, so when he arrived, he entered the basement of the apartment building. He figured she was running too many electronics, perhaps a microwave and an air conditioner at the same time that might trip a fuse. He was already aware that the wiring in the apartment was shotty, along with the rest of the apartments in the building. Shining his flashlight along the wires that led to the fuse box for her particular apartment confirmed his concerns.

Second-rate, amateur electricians had been down here a handful of times, only putting Band-aids on the huge problems this entire building has. He looked at these "Band-aids" and shook his head remembering the multiple conversations he had with the landlord who never gave a shit because he just wanted to save money while collecting even more rent from clueless tenants.

Mr. Dummy flicked the fuse that was tripped, back then forth, figuring the girl on the second floor should be all set. *Might as well call her,* he thought. Dialing her number, he figured he'd stay in the basement for a few minutes that way he doesn't have to come back if there's another problem.

"Hi, it looks like it was just a fuse issue. Does your apartment have power now?"

"Yeah."

He wasn't sure if she sounded annoyed, drunk, or both. "If you have any other issues, feel free to give me a call! This never happens unless a lot of electricity is being used at once. Do you have an air conditioner up and running yet?"

"No," she said, lying, as she stared at the air conditioner hanging on for dear life in the window. "I was using my microwave. But I've used it before and there was no issue."

"Probably just some odd, isolated incident. The building is old but I guarantee, everything is in tip-top shape!"

"Okay. Thanks."

He could feel his heart skip a beat telling the lie. But since he was down there, he'd continue to take a look around. It was darker than normal. Just one of those typical, old, dank basements that oozed with history and whatever else was creeping in the cement cracks. His flashlight hardly emphasized the weathered foundation but did a great job of showing the moisture in the walls around him. The rust colored, vein-like streaks sprinkling down the concrete led to year old drains in the floor. As well as the mouse shit sporadically spread out in multiple piles, decorating the corners of the basement.

As Mr. Dummy approached the furthest part of the basement from the entrance, he felt strange sensations on his right leg. He slapped himself, figuring it was a mosquito bite and moved on to the next corner. Aside from the fuse box, another concern he had was the gas line. *Her* apartment's stove was directly above where he was looking. No breaks, no bends. But as he got closer, it looked like there was something dripping down the entire line.

The small basement windows illuminated just a part of what was either going down—or going up—the gas line. Before leaning in for a better look, he swatted at his leg again. He scratched his skin with his dirty, broken fingernails, then rubbed his eyes to focus on what exactly was happening around him. The sensation on his leg became much more apparent, crawling up to the right side of his body. As he was trying to focus his flashlight on the gas line, his vision seemed to blur. Thinking it was the light bulb in the flash light, he shook it and then of course dropped it.

Watching it slowly roll and hitting the wall like some sort of cliché horror movie moment, he just rolled his eyes in frustration. Cursing to himself and scratching his leg even more, the bumps he felt on his leg didn't immediately concern him as he realized he just wanted to get the fuck out of this basement and back to his twelve-pack of cheap beer at home.

He picked up the flashlight and shined it on the concrete wall. Whatever he saw on the gas line was also on the wall. Glistening and reflective, what he saw was a lot...and moving fast, swarming all around him.

"What the fuck..."

Right before he touched the wall, he knew exactly what it...*they* were. He'd seen it before, being the handy man for apartments in the city for half his life. *But how could this many even happen?*

His right leg became weak. Before he knew it, his entire body felt like it was on fire. It was driving him mad, but not mad enough to know that he needed to get out. *Screw the girl upstairs. Screw the gas line, screw the electricity. Get out before the infestation follows you out to the street.*

And just like that cliché he made fun of and feared, he dropped the goddamned flashlight *again*. "Son of a bitch!"

The light from the small windows continued to dissipate as the glass became infested and covered with what he saw. The dull beam from the entrance of the basement door seemed miles away. It was just within reach when he, of course, tripped. He wasn't even surprised at himself because as bright as he wasn't, he was aware of his lack of brain power.

When his head hit the concrete floor, he got a flashback to his mother shouting at him. Yelling at how him building and fixing things doesn't hold a candle to his brother who has multiple PhDs, or some shit. His memory of his bitch of a mother distracted him from the fact that his flashlight was nowhere to be found. He started to grow angrier because he thought if he made a better salary from this joke of a landlord, he would *definitely* have had a much better quality flashlight.

Both his legs felt swollen. The sound of a million crawling legs behind him was deafening but he knew the end was in sight—the exit. He inched across the icy, basement floor with everything he had. Watching the sleeves of his flannel shirt being eaten away, losing feeling from the waist down.

The light above the basement door was almost above him. He reached toward a cement stair, but his right shoulder had been invaded, then turned from a black and red flannel shirt sleeve to a lava-like bubbling abscess of burning skin spreading to the rest of his torso.

Mr. Dummy tried to scream but then when he looked behind himself, he didn't see his body. Or his legs. Or even the basement. He only saw a nightmare of shadows. Thousands of tiny shadows eating him alive, with thousands more coming toward him. They ate away at his body while he attempted to escape this Hell that had once been just a simple basement.

The door closed. And everything went dark.

———————————

The lights flicked back on, the air conditioner hummed and the damn refrigerator sang its normal, sallow tune. The bottle of booze seemed to magically appear on the other side of the room, along with the cat, she got up and regained her balance.

"Well, I'm hungry again. Are you?" She wanted to give the cat—and the bottle—much needed attention, but all she could do was scratch. Her arms, her back…Everything just felt itchy and bumpy. Afraid of bleeding, she decided to feed the cat again, take a swig of vodka then shower.

Thus began the normal ritual of stepping down from the living room then up to the bathroom. She found herself staring in the mirror while the shower ran, the cat nearby chomping away. Engulfed with her reflection, she focused on the red abrasions going up and down her arms. She turned and pushed her hair away to examine her back. There were more hives, pulsating and red. The tiny bathroom mirror made it almost impossible for her to see everything. So, all she could do was scratch. And scratch.

She was about to let out an almost embarrassing, loud sigh of relief, when a huge *bang* echoed throughout her apartment. Instead of being startled, she took another swig of vodka, stumbled down from the bathroom, and of course, tripped *up* to the living room. Not quite falling, but wobbling, she looked down from the living room to her bedroom. She felt tall. So tall she could see the entire bedroom.

Ignoring her confusion about her new sudden height, she slowly turned to listen. Cat was still eating. Shower was still running. Naked, scratching, listening for a good minute, she heard another slam.

Oh, yeah. Mr. Dummy is probably locking up for the night. She tip-toed down to the kitchen, and peeked through the blinds to see if he was leaving. The light to the basement entrance was off, and his truck wasn't visible. Only two stories up, she could still see the rest of the dank street lit with even more depressing street lights.

The sidewalk, dirty with shadows, welcomed the drunkards and park hobos to step on the pavement. *Must have just missed him. Thanks, Mr. Dummy.* Being genuinely grateful for having the power back on, she trekked back to the shower, scratching her body until she bled.

———

Surprised to find herself suddenly half on the bed and half on the floor—along with the cat—she knew she could also ignore her hangover by organizing the strange closet that attracted her to the apartment in the first place.

But first, coffee! The cat basically shrugged as she announced her plans, but he followed her down from the bedroom, up to the living room and down to the kitchen.

"What in the hell...?"

The coffee maker lay shattered on the kitchen floor. She immediately blamed the cat.

"Well, it didn't just slide off the counter, did it?" *No. There's no way he could have knocked over the whole thing. Plus, it didn't even wake me up. I don't remember either of us getting up in the middle of the night. Shit. I'm losing my fucking mind in this fucking place.*

She quickly fed the cat, swept up the glass, and went outside for a walk and a coffee. *Fuck the closet!*

It was warm out and abnormally bright. She could breathe again. The ground was flat and even and lovely. The vertigo or whatever she had been feeling seemed to wither away with each step. Or maybe it was sobriety. *Nahhh*! Since it was past noon, she finished her coffee and went to the liquor store.

She folded clothes and put them back on the crooked shelves in the closet, starting to feel uneasy. Perhaps because she hadn't started drinking vodka yet. She pulled the string to turn off the halfcocked light bulb and slowly walked out of the closet. Which she now decided she didn't like anymore. It was too narrow. Too odd. Like everything else in this fucking place.

The days were supposed to be getting longer but whenever she was inside the apartment, everything seemed to get darker quicker. She had never thanked Mr. Dummy for fixing the electricity problem from last night so she went to shoot him a quick text.

"Well, how about we eat first?"

The cat seemed to be startled by her enthusiasm and jumped off the bed in a frenzy and ran to the kitchen. Oblivious, she agreed to herself and to him.

She went to grab the bottle when the lights started to dim. Then flicker. Which was confusing because she wasn't even using the microwave this time. She found herself in the kitchen, seeing the cat in between flashes of light. On. His terrified face. Off. Darkness. She slowly started to panic and opened one of the windows to let the familiar street lights come in. But nothing.

The cat was looking behind her. He had seen all this the entire time they had lived there, but typically only when she was sleeping. There was a darkness coming, crawling toward the both of them.

The cat started pacing back and forth to the entrance of the kitchen and back to the window she opened.

"What is it, bub? It's okay! It's just the damn fuses again."

The flickering lights brightened the path toward her phone and the bottle on the nightstand next to her bed. Up from the kitchen.

Down from the living room. Up to the bedroom. *This is still a one floor apartment. Not sure why this is still happening.* She grabbed the bottle and took a nice, long sip, becoming more and more pissed off because Mr. Dummy was supposed to have fixed the situation.

The lights went completely out. Her cell phone screen turned on and illuminated just a tiny bit of the bedroom. She took another sip, letting the liquid warm her insides.

"Jesus Christ." She reached for the phone, absolutely cringing at the thought of bothering Mr. Dummy *again* for the same reason.

Her feet started burning. The nerves in her toes felt electrified, flesh to bone. She turned around and jumped so fast, the phone still plugged into the wall ripped out. The charger nearly missed her temple, and of course she, fell, twisted and half in the bedroom, half in the entrance to the living room. She laughed.

The cat poked its head around from the kitchen. His eyes absorbed on what was behind her, terrified while he watched.

With one hand holding her phone, the other grasping the bottle, she attempted to get back up in the dark. Her feet began to burn even more. She threw her phone across the apartment and screamed so loud, derelicts in the park heard the sound from the open window in her bedroom. The cat ran to the other side of the kitchen.

Down from the bedroom. Up to the living room.

She looked back to the swarming bedroom, knowing right then and there why she had always been so itchy. The red bumps infesting her skin weren't a fucking allergy.

The crooked TV fell over, and the outlet plates popped off their own screws. The off-white walls became darker. Everything was crawling. Including her. She used her elbows and forearms to move, ignoring the fact that her hips now started to sear with pain.

Up and across the living room. She was too afraid to look back, but she did anyway. They were crawling out of the mattress, out of the bedroom lamp, swarming from her toes to her ankles. Then to her knees. The few that already got to her hips were inviting their friends for more. *Is this it? Is this the moment I am going to die?*

The walls around her started to pulsate. She plunged ahead on her palms, dragging herself to the kitchen.

The cat was backed up in the corner, beneath the open window. He knew this was it as well. They had never really bothered him, only her. But they were devouring everything in sight.

The pain she experienced was inexplicable. The burning sensation went from her hips to her chest. She couldn't even feel her legs anymore. If she could get to the open window, she'd be home free. The closer she got, the more freaked out the cat was. She reached an arm out, but the cat jumped to the window sill. He looked outside, then back in, his tail twitching in despair.

She didn't want to, but she looked back again. At this point, it was just shadows of them. The gleaming light from the street lamp shone through the kitchen window and revealed the true horror of what was actually happening to her. Her legs were gone. The bloodied knubs were getting devoured while everything else continued being covered by crawling darkness. She still felt like she couldn't give up.

Down from the living room. Up to the kitchen.

Her back now seared with an itch she could not scratch. Her skin bubbled, being invaded. The red bumps that once were, broke open into bloody orifices that welcomed them—the ones who had made the wounds. And now they were finishing it. She wanted to cry, but couldn't. She wanted to escape, but couldn't. It was like the entire nightmare apartment was coming to life. It confirmed her doubts at that coffee shop. It was confirmed her instincts from the first night she had spent here, confirming the weird walls and floors.

The crooked apartment. The crooked landlord. And the crooked, missing-in-action, Mr. Dummy.

"Let's meet at the coffee shop to go over the lease."

"It's available immediately. Immediately. IMMEDIATELY."

"Will you have cash or check? CASH OR CHECK?"

Down to the kitchen.

She looked back again. Then turned to her cat.

"Go!"

As she yelled, she pushed herself forward. They were up to her shoulders. The fridge stopped shuddering. The kitchen was painted black. And just as her arms and face withered away, the cat jumped out the window.

He landed on his feet onto the cold sidewalk. The cat looked up and watched the apartment windows go dark.

And so did she.

How Does a Dead Girl Call for Help?

He fucked her on a stained mattress. Her limp, lifeless body bobbed up and down while he continued to thrust. The mattress looked old and worn, blemished with brown discolorations and who knows what else.

I was completely powerless, figuring he would move on to me like he had with her. But he didn't. I was gone the minute his hands were around my throat, taking my last breath, then all I saw was black. My heart stopped beating, my lungs stopped working, and I was prepared to go somewhere else. Or nowhere at all. But I remained stuck inside this shell of a body, for some reason, still watching him.

I found myself pretending to be dead. But I was already dead. There was no fear, and I felt nothing. Not physically, anyway. But I could still see, think, and hear. I continued to stare through eyes that were probably losing color.

If I were capable of feeling anything at this moment, it would have been mostly confusion. If I was dead, why could I still think? Why could I still hear and see what was going on around me?

After he was done, he looked over at me and caressed my body. He began to undress me so carefully, like he was taking care of a sick child, his pupils big and dark. It was like he could hardly contain himself. Two bodies in bed with him. He then pushed the other girl onto the floor and left the room for what I guessed to be a few minutes. But when you're dead, time is meaningless. I stared at the ceiling and tried to move.

How does a dead girl call for help? Technically, I don't need help any more.

He came back with a dress in his hands and just stood over me. The garment was off-white and dingy, like it had long ago belonged on a child at a christening. Or on an adult during her wedding night in the 1800's. The man slipped the dress on my body, placing his hands everywhere. He just couldn't help himself. Like a sick-fuck child in a candy store.

"You're mine forever," he said.

With everything happening right now, what was more inexplicable was watching someone touch me and not feel it. I couldn't express my disgust, couldn't call out, couldn't get up and run.

He then put his arm around me and fell asleep. Over and over, the air whistled from his nose, snorting out of his mouth like a hog in heat. All I wanted to do was choke the life out of him like he had done to me.

I was still attempting to process my thoughts. Apparently, that's all I had left. I wanted to blink or move my fingers. Anything! But nothing happened. I couldn't move my head, so I concentrated on the ceiling, figuring if I tried, I could maybe lift my arm. Still nothing. The stiffness of being dead felt number than numb. It was like that moment when your foot "falls asleep" and starts to cramp up, but then you wiggle your ankle and toes. That moment in between the cramping and feeling the cramping stop—is what it feels like to be dead.

While he lay next to me, I contemplated my next move.

The room was still dark when my arm moving awoke him.

He grabbed my head and turned my face toward his, confirming that I was in fact, still dead. The man stared into my eyes. I assumed he had just figured he was half asleep. Though, he was absolutely right. My arm *did* move.

———————————

I was still on the bed when the room grew brighter and he awoke. The bleeding, other dead girl on the floor was starting to smell. I only knew because he talked to himself. He left the room, but his feet dragging and shuffling, echoed throughout the house, or wherever I was, like a haunted inn. Was this a joke? Was I going to be here forever? This disgusting room and this disgusting man, my gravesite? Doors or cabinets squeaked open and slammed shut, then he eventually reappeared.

He began to mop up the parts of the other girl, which were sprinkled about all over the dilapidated floor. It was difficult for him to ignore the enormous hard-on he had while trying to move the mop. Apparently, he was so turned on by the entrails and blood, he stopped, threw the cleaning products on the ground, and grabbed his dick. He fell to floor and went at it. It must have lasted less than thirty seconds. I don't know if it was the pleasure he felt in between the blood, the bleach, and the mop, but it clearly must have been so intense, that afterward, he lay on the linoleum, dick still in hand, staring at the wall like a thirteen-year-old boy.

The room continued to get brighter, even though the sunlight hardly broke through the curtains caked in dust. They were even more stained than the mattress itself. Eventually, he cleaned himself off, then dragged the other girl out of the room. I was still on the bed. If I had really been able to move my arm during the night, could I, a dead person, move off this damn bed? I would have liked to say I felt worry or panic, but mostly, I just wondered where he had taken the other dead girl. And if he was going to bring me to where she went next. Would he jerk off on me too? Or worse?

Oh, that's right. I was dead. It wasn't going to get any worse.

An unknown amount of time later, he grabbed my ankles and pulled me off the bed. I heard the *thump* of my head and upper body hitting the floor before he dragged me across the room. He sat me up against the wall and started positioning me like a doll. The man cracked my arms together, making sure my fingers were entwined and proper. My hips popped when he crossed my legs. When he got my body just like he wanted, he started combing my hair.

"Perfect. My perfect little girl," he said, getting a quick breast fondle. He started to unbutton the dress I was wearing but stopped and stared into my face. His were empty. Demonic. His pupils began to grow and blacken, like a cat's when ready to kill.

A shuffling sound reverberated outside the room, interrupting his plans, and he opened the door I was propped up against. He shoved me inside a closet like a child would do with a toy they are done playing with. The shuddered door, wooden and rotting, allowed me to see bits of the room I had just been in. Was this all I would have to look at ever again? He couldn't keep me around forever. My parts were going to start rotting off. Then again, I couldn't even look at myself, only toward where my head was facing—a slave to the surroundings.

Eventually, I heard voices in the background, but they were too muffled for me to distinguish the actual words. So, I just stared through the closet doors until everything became too dark to see. The stiffening seemed to lessen, and my hips gave. The top part of my body shifted to the ground. The *thump* from my shoulder hitting the floor blew away dust, letting it escape underneath the closet door. I could still make out the room, as black as it was, and a faint light from outside illuminated the dull, cracked ground. The dust settled and a spider crawled by. As time went on, all I had to do was stare at that fucking floor.

Suddenly the bedroom door violently swung open, and a light flicked on. There was a woman shrieking and crying, a *thwack* sound, then no more screaming. The cracks in the closet doors allowed me to see very little, other than his pacing boots and the dirtied box spring sitting on the ground. He moved to the top of the bed, and red splattered onto the floor like spiderwebs flinging through space before turning into puddles on the ground. Air escaped through a gurgling throat, slightly muffling the sound of a belt unbuckling.

Then, the familiar squeaking of the mattress moving back and forth...Between the clamor of the bed and the cacophony of his moans, I couldn't help but wonder how much longer this all would go on for. The blood on the floor turned from red to brown, and the box spring stopped singing its twisted tune.

Eventually, the closet doors recklessly opened. A light shined on the dusty floor I had been staring at. Was he in a rush all of a sudden? He dumped the woman's body in the far corner of the closet. His half-naked body crouched, and he reached toward mine. He propped me up again, lifting my pelvis forward so I was slouched against the wall. My left arm bounced from the floor to his face. Did I do that? Did I try to hit him, or was it that pesky gravity? He ignored my arm, kissed my forehead, then jumped out of the closet and ran from the room.

This time, however, the closet door was left open.

Was he getting sloppy? Or *sloppier*? The room was once again dark. I watched myself plop back to the ground, this time with a squish. How long had it really been? My eyes were at the floor, reunited with the dust.

The more and more I continued to stare at the dirty hardwood, the more it started to blur out of focus. It reverberated in front of my eyes, like it was taunting me. The distortion then evolved into a blinding white. Instinctually, I attempted to cover my eyes with my hand. But then I remembered...

Flashes of the bright light and darkness were weaving back and forth with my sight. I saw the curtains in the room, then a hallway. Blackness muddied my vision while the light reached out to bring it all back. My sight zoomed in and out, able to once again focus. My head must have been tilted down. I was able to see my chest, the top of my legs, and cheap linoleum. This linoleum looked like it belonged in a kitchen from fifty years ago. Tiled, probably once white, green, and orange. Now appearing rust-colored. The squares and obscure designs were scuffed with years of abuse and a lack of upkeep. I was thinking how great it was to be staring at yet another floor, when a key was thrusted into a lock and a door opened.

"What the fuck?" The man's brown boots appeared before me. He kneeled and used his finger to move my chin up.

We met eyes. His pupils were tiny this time. His finger and thumb moved my head back and forth as if he was trying to figure it all out.

I'm still dead, you idiot.

He hurried away from me, leaving my head to drop back where it was. My jaw unhinged, mouth open. His footsteps resonated throughout the walls of my confinement. The roar of his stomping feet decreased, and I returned to looking at the hideous floor. The flicker of white light started to come back, when it was interrupted by the increased volume of his footsteps.

In front of me once again, he leaned down. With his head on my lap, he began to sob. His arms reached around my abdomen, and he pulled himself closer, howling like a lost child screaming for his mother. The wet sounds of him snuffing the snot back into his nostrils repulsed me. After everything I had seen and heard, my disgust swelled. The blackness and white light began to flicker when the man's head moved closer to mine.

He began to nuzzle my chest, squeezing my back tighter and tighter with his hands. His dirty-blond hair, matted with thick, greasy sweat, almost blocked my vision and pressed against my jaw. His scalp cuddled against my chin, which forced my face closer to the top of his skull. A loud clamping sound transpired, making my ears ring. He screamed the typical blood-curdling cry. My teeth had chomped down through his hair and skin, spraying blood all over the cheap-looking kitchen floor. At first, I was confused about what was happening. Why was he was screaming like a little girl at the sight of his own blood?

My jaw unclenched, then bit down again. The sound of bone tearing through bone was inexplicable. Pieces of spongey brain shot to the back of my throat, while more blood spewed in every direction. I had him locked. His arms waved, legs fluttering—and of course, dick hard.

Eventually, the gurgling stopped. He had choked on his own blood. His sputtering body continued to convulse, the last few death ticks of his body ending the violent jolts of motion. My jaw still stayed clenched, teeth gripping what was left of his scalp, skull, and brain.

His flesh snapped from my mouth with a slap, and his body fell to the floor. Dead and bloody.

The white light began its vibration again and slowly turned into an infinite darkness. I had the answer to my question: how does a dead girl call for help?

She takes what was taken from her.

Life.

Yes, Chef!

"Vegans are almost as ridiculous as Christians!" he screamed at the server.

That was one of the many things he couldn't stand. Gluten-free this, vegetarian that...It was like the whole world was turning into one giant pussy. One giant pussy that might swallow him whole—and not in a good way. People used to listen to him. People used to follow his lead and cook exactly how he directed.

Fine dining was a fine movie. No need for the Oscars. He was once upon a time a three-star Michelin chef. Now he just tried to carry what little sanity he had left. It was buried in his bitterness and disgust. He would never identify as anything like a sociopath, though he would like to label himself that. But if he did, it would have been a far cry from the sad, old man who was losing his grip. Not on the knife, though. Never the knife.

Whether it was organic, halal, farm-to-table, he never had a problem with it. Meat is meat and that is what humans need. Humans are natural hunters, natural killers. And they all need to eat to live. Animals were just his catalyst. They always had been. He never respected them because he was the master and they were the pathetic prey he used for beautiful dishes idiots will pay top dollar for. If he used a ridiculous garnish, they'd pay even more. But hey, if it's tasty and it's pretty and looks good on social media, he knew he'd always be guaranteed good reviews, great resume updates, and eventually a future that would let him retire.

Or so he thought.

When your career becomes more important than your own life, you think you surpass it, then the arrogance of this becomes God.

"What's your specialty?" He always laughed at this question. And that question got asked a lot. However, he had traveled all over the world, cooked for people even more arrogant than himself. And yet...the animals. He made them his bitch, ignoring his failed marriages and the countless affairs he'd had. *They all look up to me. They all owe me. They all need to listen to me!* He used legal rifles to kill deer, and illegal handguns for fun.

The chef had fucked countless bartenders and waitresses, pretending he actually mattered in someone else's life. But the animals. The animals. He has skinned and boned them. He has boiled them, braised them. The women he had been with were just a step up from animals. They were the ones who had been "allowed" to let his dick enter them. But either way, most of it all tasted better with butter and deglazed with white wine on a pan. Preferably, cast iron. It is obviously the best. He knew this. He also knew everyone and everything around him was just pathetic.

Until he cooked lobster one night.

The last few years of his first marriage, she had known. Wife #1 had always been self-conscious and suspicious, but her love for him had blinded her. Though, she was not an idiot. He knew this, and he had also managed to use her loyalty to his advantage. He spread the loyalty out and used it like some lame deconstructed sushi dish. Or the pathetic seafood pasta she had begged him to make for her. He rarely bothered.

Even though she would "attempt" to make dinner on the many days he was working, he would just become more annoyed. If he came home early, he'd educate her on how to chop an onion or criticize the mediocre recipes she was using. She had really just wanted to surprise him, let him relax and eat some "okay" food. But that wasn't a possibility, apparently. He would just nitpick and even ridicule the way she held a knife. *Jesus, you lefties are almost like Democrats. Trying to fix shit with the wrong tools!*

This went on for years. She had finally found the multiple pictures from young co-workers of his who were more than spreadeagle, along with messages she feared. All from the skinny, little waitresses he always had been around. She also finally realized his disgusting "thing" for bartenders and left him.

As did the next wife. And the next one. It was literally a recipe he had created. Again and again. Find a pretty girl. Find a pretty girl. Then sprinkle with more pretty girls, generously. Salt and pepper, spices and vices. What was strange, is all of his wives loved animals. They had absolutely not been vegan, but they always had soft spots for dogs and cats and deer...He would scowl as they would become upset at the sight of a dead raccoon—or whatever—on the side of the road. Chef laughed at every single one of their hypocrisies. *You eat meat! Why the sympathy? It's fucking weakness, you idiot!*

They did all leave *him*. His ultimate numbness and stubbornness killed each relationship. He didn't understand the "freak out" which occurred when he'd stomp on spiders or shoot chipmunks with the BB gun. *Who gives a fuck! It's just a moth.* Or *Who gives a shit. It's a mole ruining the yard!* He didn't care because he knew almost anything he killed could be a plate.

"I'll garnish your ass with parsley, like an amateur!" he'd yell this while he drank his cheap beers and even cheaper whiskey. When he was too drunk and missed a chipmunk or two, he'd notice them looking back at him. Like they were mocking him. *Haha nice shot, fucker, try and make us into a stock! See you in stew hell!* He'd never forget those looks, shooting a few more times and missing. That sad, condescending look in their eyes, like his first wife always had. In fact, even like his second and third wives. Like they *knew* he'd be wrong. Like they *knew* he'd miss the shot. It was like those mundane animals and his silly ex-wives were the same species, predicting when he would fail. But how could he fail?

Almost every night before passing out, he'd reminisce about recipes he mastered, *still* feeling superior, while disregarding and ignoring his past mistakes. *Mistakes? I make none.* He watched a rabbit hop by. Chef started to aim the ol' faithful BB gun but tripped over his own drunken self. His head bounced off the wooden porch, but he was able to hold on to his beer. He laughed, and started to get up, then attempted to focus. Chef admired the callouses between his thumb and pointer finger, then decided to ignore the minor bite-like marks on his arms and legs, which were scabbing over quite nicely. He ignored them, mostly because he didn't remember where they had come from.

"You know, you *really* don't have to kill those squirrels. Or rabbits. Or whatever the hell it is you're doing. It's not like they're doing any damage," Wife #3 had said.

He gripped the gun tight and crushed his beer can into a flat disk. Chef threw it on to the uncut grass with such disregard, she had known it was a metaphor for his feelings toward her. She had hardly spent time with him for the last two weeks. But his arrogance had never allowed him to feel guilt. Plus, he was too busy worrying about specials for the upcoming week, along with the new bartender he planned on banging in the walk-in. *She's worrying about squirrels while I'm worrying about what positions I haven't tried on top of the bins of spinach. Pathetic. She could be hot, but we're married. Boring. Like grilled chicken. She could be more fuckable, but she isn't trying to make a living by sucking up to customers. Or wanting to suck them off. HAHA!*

He'd started to think about staff meal, which also meant he had to worry about how long it was going to take him to get off with the new bartender so the rest of the wait staff wouldn't realize what was going on in the walk-in.

Wife #3 had to interrupt his thoughts by asking if he was okay. *Why even bother, bitch?* She had looked at him with legitimate concern. Then a gopher had run up to the porch, sniffing at the leaves and seeds on the ground. Chef stared at it, thinking the animal looked like a pork butt begging to be marinated and slow cooked for Cubano sandwiches. He pictured the orange slices and limes...the rump just perfect when he grabbed his rifle and aimed...

"What the fuck!"

She hadn't been able to stop him. He already pulled the trigger. The gopher was hit on its side, then ran away.

"Almost killed the fucker! Hah!" *I actually probably did...*

"What the hell is wrong with you?"

She had already known the answer to her question. She always knew what he was going to say. He was "blowing off steam." It was his "way of relaxing after working 14 hours." He wanted to "get his mind off work" for a minute. Leave him alone. Stop bitching. Blah blah blah. The realization why she was his third wife was now apparent, becoming her lucky epiphany.

He turned around and looked at her with empty eyes. He was not only drunk, self-loathing, full of hate, and high on a kill...but he was *still* thinking about work. She had thought he was going to hit her. He's only hit a woman once. The second wife. That little indiscretion had gotten him a scar. Just another to go along with his collection of work-related ones. *Oops...* he had started laughing out loud, thinking about it, fully aware of what a jackass he can be. Chef was amused for a second but then he looked back around, becoming more furious at the sight of her.

His words slurred as he finished off his ninth beer. "Don't try annnd cut me like the other...the other one! Bitches! You're all bitches! Jeethus chri-i-ist, why am I even wif you?"

He stumbled toward her as she walked inside. She could smell his hot breath, wet with stale beer. The door had almost hit his face, but he hardly noticed.

"Ahh, fuck ya!" He clutched the empty beer can, wondering where his gun had gone. His ears starting ringing in unison with crickets chirping in the background. Which would have made sense to him, but he had forgotten it was almost summer. It was swamp-like, abnormal, and echoed into deafness. *Well, I'm definitely fucked up*, he thought.

"You know what?" Wife #3 raised her voice, "Fuck *you*! I'm not sure how anything we've ever shared together has meant this little to you, so that's fine. But what baffles my fucking mind is that you *still* think you are above everyone else, including that fucking gopher. Fuck you!"

As always, his self-importance—and stubbornness—had shined through. He knew everything he did was done better than everyone else. Chef would pretend to care for a few seconds when people complemented his dishes, just so his ego could be stroked. He had already known they are great. But these animals...These damn animals just didn't seem to give a shit about his feelings. Which was odd, because it had been something he just couldn't comprehend. It was like his job and his talent and his ego were untouchable. He would come home late at night, lonely, exhausted, but still somehow feel superior to whatever human, animal...because he *just knew* he was better. He couldn't be proved wrong because he was *never* wrong. *Never.*

He sat down on his shoddy, vinyl camping chair—the cheap kind from a discount store that usually broke after sitting on it once. The plastic legs sank from his weight and scratched the wood of the back deck. Eventually, the chirping of the crickets had dissipated, the wind stopped blowing, and the lightning bugs flickered throughout the yard. He slowly passed out from inebriation.

Oblivious to the fact that a pair of eyes were coming toward him—small, glowing red, and angry.

Wife #3 slept on the couch that night. Two weeks later, she was the last wife that was gone for good.

Chef awoke from one of his many slumbers, forgetting about one of his many dream-like memories involving one of his many wives, and feeling slightly depressed. And very hungover. He followed the trail of empty beer bottles and cans to the bathroom, where he noticed the back door was wide open. *Whathefuckever.* He knew he had to piss, then cure his hangover with beer for breakfast. *Venison sausage for breakfast too? Fuck yeah.*

The side of his head was pounding, his urine so yellow it was practically orange. He tried to ignore the fact his first wife would always try and get him to drink more water. Or had it been the third? He stopped himself from thinking about it because it was just giving him more of a headache than he already had. Chef stepped forward to flush. His one foot still wearing a sock from the night before stepped in a warm puddle. His bare foot remained dry. The bathroom smelled of mold and stale piss, the walls yellowed from years of smoking. Chef knew he must have stepped in urine, but instead of showering, he threw his one sock in the trash.

He grabbed a half-drunk beer on the stand near the back door and took a nice big swig. As he started to close the door and actually lock it this time, he noticed something run through the high brush by the trees. A fox, maybe even a coyote perhaps.

"Better not be a gopher, you prick!" He shed the memories from his brain that had woken him up and chugged the rest of a semi-flat, day-old beer. Chef slammed the door shut and was ready to create another masterpiece. Breakfast for him, by him—something he rarely did.

This time he made *sure* the back door was closed and locked.

After he plated his food and drank his second morning beer, the hangover withered away. Between a buzz and a realization, between the *fuck this* and *fuck that* of his thoughts, Chef considered taking a picture of his "simple" breakfast. Not knowing where his phone was, he decided to ignore his own art, ignore the fact he probably had half a million texts from his line cook, and just fucking eat. He chewed, stuffing himself like a savage, and washed down each sloppy swallow with another sip of skunky beer. Chef wasn't sure if he was getting drunk again or just drinking himself sober.

He sat at his crooked kitchen table, and his leg started to sear in pain. Itchy. Again. But just like most moments that might actually mean something, he ignored it.

———————————

Chef began to think back about a couple of months ago, at his restaurant. It had been a late night—at least that's what he told Wife #3. He planned on banging the new server, who was into being humiliated by authoritative men. A lot of servers were always over sharing.

They were like that, all of them the same, throughout his entire career: chatty and easy. This one had just the right personality trait he used to his advantage.

During closing, he had taken her behind the dumpster. *Damn what was her name? Ah well*, he thought. While she was giving him mediocre head, he had seen these red eyes staring at him through some bushes behind the parking lot. It was only for a split second he had noticed it. He was a little pre-occupied at the moment to even care. Before getting to the crucial climax, he had opened his eyes back up and watched the red eyes getting closer to them.

He pushed the server away, mostly out of frustration. The distraction of whatever he had seen wasn't letting him finish.

"What the hell, *chef*?"

He didn't appreciate her sarcastic tone and also didn't enjoy the interruption by some animal that was lurking around. Before she could ask what was wrong with him—she distinctly witnessed worry on his face—he told her to fuck off.

"It wasn't that good. I'm just gonna go home and get the job done myself. You should do the same."

She was pissy, but kept her mouth shut and walked away as he adjusted himself. He started to walk back into the restaurant buckling his belt into place, when a large raccoon had run up to him and sank its teeth into Chef's non-slip shoes.

Motherfucker. I don't remember her name, but I definitely remember that. His leg started burning again. On his third morning beer, his thoughts became interrupted. He decided to go outside to his backyard when he saw his phone on the decrepit patio table. Brushing off the leaves and whatever else the wind brought throughout the night, he sat down at the patio to smoke and drink his beer. Quickly looking at his phone, he had a few missed calls and multiple texts but he wasn't ready to read them. This was his one and only day off, refusing to be "on call" anymore. He finished the third beer with a hearty chug and his phone started ringing again.

Todd, you useless son of a bitch.

"Yeah?" He let out a belch after answering Todd's call, surprised Todd couldn't smell it through the phone.

"Chef? Chef! I am so, so sorry to bother you. But there's a big fucking problem here. Sir."

"There's always a goddamn problem. It's the business." He waited for Todd's response, uncaring and wondering if it was time for a fourth beer.

Ka-ting! He lifted the phone away from his ear, but he knew what it was. Todd had definitely thrown a pan at something.

"Chef! Produce didn't come in this morning! Which means we have absofuckinglutely no potatoes for mash. *Then! Then!* The goddamn hood fan broke. Or something! It's not working! Then to top it all off, Amanda and Courtney got into some cat fight about who didn't roll silverware last night! I swear to shit, none of this happens when *you're* here!"

There's that ego stroke.

"Is that all?" he asked, clearly annoyed.

"Yes. Chef."

"Todd, you really make me question why I hired you in the first place. Screw Amanda and Courtney, I could care less if they have a knife fight in the dining area with each other. Let those bitches cry it out and get back to work when service starts. In fact, have one of them go to The Depot and grab a ten-pound bag of Russets. Call Jeff, his card is in my office on the whiteboard. He's usually on call for Saturdays. Have him fix that fucking hood vent, I don't care what he has to do."

"Yes, Chef."

"Anything else? Or do I have to continue to hold your hand?"

"Well…" Todd trailed off.

"Jesus Christ, *what*?"

"The produce order. What if it doesn't come in? Won't we be fucked until next week?"

Chef could hear the fear in Todd's voice. Todd should have been afraid, because it was a dumb- ass question.

"Call Food-Co! Place another order online if you have to!" He hung up on Todd, suspecting he might get another call later on when dinner service starts. *Shoemaker.* He knew the babies would figure it out, so he turned off his phone and went inside to fetch another beer.

———————

Chef woke up a few hours later. It was still daylight, but something was wrong. His back ached, and his legs and ass burned. He rubbed the crust out of his eyes and gained his composure, realizing the chair broke right underneath him. If his neck hadn't been so bent and mangled from sleeping in this monstrosity, he would have laughed. He lifted himself up by his palms, but even his elbows were sore. The deck was soiled with soot and humidity, the air thicker than the asshole of Hell.

Shower time. How many beers do I have left?

Walking back into the house felt like glass scraping his toes to the bone. Each step was gravel to his shins, but the first priority was washing his nasty ass. He didn't know how long he had slept during the mid-morning to afternoon after the phone call with idiot Todd, but as he was getting lost in his thoughts in the shower, he looked down at his feet. The water washed away the grime and dirt and …*blood?*

The hot water started washing away bits of soggy flesh from his toes and feet. For a split second, he watched chewed-off pieces of skin go down the drain. Then, he turned off the water. Chef sat on the edge of the tub and examined both his feet. Each had multiple indents and contusions. *Teeth marks?* He looked at his legs, remembering the scabbing and comparing it to these fresh, bloody wounds on his feet. The scabs were larger, almost like a chain of quarter-sized pockmarks, while the mess on his feet were tiny, razor-sharp little bites from...*some kind of animal?* He became angrier. Chef grabbed the first aid kit from his junk drawer, another beer, then confirmed both his BB gun and rifle were up against the wall near his back door. Confusion and paranoia, mixed with a day-and-a-half bender, created a cocktail of sloppily bandaged feet.

He stumbled back outside, staring at the yard. Two squirrels twitched their tails while digging at the ground. The more their tails twitched, the more his feet hurt and bled into his sloppy bandages. Chef slowly put down his beer and aimed his rifle at the squirrel to the right. He looked through the scope, matched up the crosshairs to the squirrel's head, and fired.

"Haha!" He was in disbelief he managed to pulverize half of the squirrel's body.

Miraculously, the other one ran away, not catching any of the crossfire.

The summer sun was just starting to set. He stood like a wanna-be soldier with his guns and beers, listening to the earsplitting sounds of cicadas. Sweat and beer leaked from his pores, and he asked himself if he was losing it or not. *Do all chefs reach a certain age where they want to give up? Do they look back with regret and dread for the future? Or do they stand around drunk in their backyards, ignoring the duties of tomorrow and waiting for something to kill? Fuck it.*

He staggered inside, letting the backdoor slam shut, and carefully placed the rifle—and BB gun—against the wall. Chef thought about ordering pizza, or maybe some fried chicken, but his stomach wrenched and gurgled at the thought of food. He had to go back to work tomorrow, so he nibbled on the morning's sausage that had been left on the stovetop all day. The acid in his stomach sizzled some more, so he found a bag of chips, chugged his last beer, and passed out once again.

But this time on his bed, as opposed to a broken chair outside.

———————————

"Rough night?" Todd asked. He was annoyingly observant.

Then again, it was obvious. Chef limped through the kitchen. His feet throbbed and probably smelled like pus, but luckily, his work shoes smelled like work shoes and concealed that. His work pants chafed against the wounds on his legs, tearing off the scabs. The new wounds, however, were on his face.

When he had woke up that morning, it looked like a treasure trail of deep-red grazes starting from the top of his cheek, ending at the middle of his neck. Cleaning it out with the hydrogen peroxide housed in a dusty bottle in his bathroom had seemed to do the trick, but he had to cover it up with gauze anyhow.

"Yeah. Fuck me."

"All right. So, everything is prepped for service. Monica is covering for Amanda because she had...something, I don't fucking know. Jose clocked in early, as we have 160 on the books tonight. He's double-checking the plates right now."

"Great," Chef said looking at his reflection and analyzing the marks on his face he hadn't managed to cover with the bandaging. For the first time in decades, he didn't give a shit about his job. Or the food. Or the service.

"Ohhhkaythen…" Todd said in one breath.

"What? *Jesus*. I fell asleep on an old chair and it broke. Too many beers and not enough pussy. Did the lobsters come in?"

"Yeah. Crates are in the walk-in, Jose is also getting the stock pots ready."

When service began, Chef missed the days of doing lines with his old sous in the back, energized and ready for anything. The yelling, the *clink-clanking* of dishes, a hostess he didn't recognize running back and forth, Todd scampering about like a wounded retard missing a limb…the burning butter on the fiftieth pan broke his day dreaming—and his concentration.

"Chef. Chef. *Chef*!" Todd yelled. He and Monica were standing there, staring at Chef's bleeding face, watching the droplets fall into the burnt butter.

"Fuck. Just re-fire this." Calmly, Chef grabbed the two huge lobsters, plopped them in the boiling water, and took five while Todd finished the sauce.

I burnt the butter? What an amateur. He wiped the sweat from his brow with an already dirty kitchen towel. He started to dry his face, almost forgetting the bloody craters on his cheek. There were only a few tables of people left, so he snuck to the guest bathroom. It had better lighting so he could reassess the damage. It was slow now, and the end of the night, so even if he was MIA for a few minutes, idiot Todd and the rest of the kids could—hopefully—handle it. There were a few live lobsters left in the walk-in. The two he threw in the water were cooking to death. He started to get hard just thinking about them dying, when low and behold, Monica walked in on him. Chef began to peel away the face bandages, but Monica locked the door behind her.

Aside from her giving him a quick rub in the walk-in a few weeks back, he hadn't given her one lick of a thought, except for when shouting orders were ready. She ignored the half-peeled bandages on his face and went straight for his belt. He leaned up against the sink, thinking this was just what he needed. Screw the pains in his body. Screw this job. He just needed a release, and that would get him square.

His dick didn't even get wet before she shrilled and shrieked, like a little girl seeing a ghost. His pants were down to his ankles, and before he was able to see what she had seen, Monica ran out of the bathroom. *Wow, what the hell is the matter with that bitch? Never see a dick befo—*

The cuts, or bitemarks, or whatever they were on his legs were bleeding again. The blood snaked down from each gaping wound. He wasn't sure if he was bleeding to death or losing his mind. Once again being robbed from getting—probably—mediocre head, he grabbed paper towels, sopped up what leaking liquids he could, pulled up his pants and left the restaurant.

There was only a two-top left. Todd and the bunch still have it covered. Right?

Chef opened the door to his truck and saw a thick fish tub in his passenger's seat. Todd had even made sure to slice holes on the top. *Ahh, yes.* Tomorrow is a holiday, and he became excited. He drove to the store for more beer, realizing he could cook lobster, eat, and drink like a savage, then jerk off in the shower afterward. Trying to forget about what didn't happen in the bathroom, he slammed down a 24-rack, hydrogen peroxide, and a box of adhesive bandages. The giant ones.

"You okay?" the pimply cashier asked. He kept staring at the still half-peeled bandages on Chef's face, which exposed the craters that were starting to pool up with blood again.

"How much?"

"Forty-three twenty-five."

"Jesus." Chef handed the young cashier his card. His face was a mess too.

"Are you a cook?"

His white jacket covered in a variety of red and brown stains—some actual food, some his own blood at this point.

"No." He grabbed his card back and struggled to put it back in his wallet. "I'm a chef."

————————————

He sat parked in the driveway to his house, finishing up a road beer. Chef crinkled up the can, ready to throw it near the garbage bin. He noticed a few stray crushed beer cans he had previously thrown—and missed—along with various cigarette butts strewn about. This small section up against his house looked like a mixture of some trailer park trash site and one of the literal over-filled dumpsters at a restaurant. It smelled of hot garbage, stale beer, and piss, all eating away at what grass was left growing on the ground.

*Only thing about a woman not being here anymore, it sure did look and smell better. Probably should hire some cheap, whore housekeeper...*Chef felt sorry for himself for the first time in over twenty years. He cracked open a beer, grabbed his tub of lobsters, and walked inside to his dark, dank little abode.

Chef ignored the beer bottles attracting flies all throughout his kitchen and living room. He threw the tub of lobsters in his greasy fridge. When he opened the freezer, he panicked, but a calm washed over him as he saw his frosted plastic pint of half-drunk whiskey. Next to a fresh, unopened pack of smokes.

He chugged the whiskey like he was in a desert, quenching his thirst with the most delicious water he had ever had. That was the thing about cheap whiskey—it had that beautiful burn from tongue to throat, coating your esophagus and warming your chest and belly. He had to chase it with beer, though. The aftertaste was unbearable.

Ready for a smoke, he walked toward the back of his house when...*Shit.*

"What in the fuck?" He huffed in confusion, seeing his back door wide open *again*.

His face, feet, and legs—everything—hurt. But now the booze and anger were kicking in, he was figuring Wife #3 must have been messing with him. They had all been crazy, but since she was the most recent one, could she be doing this? He'd changed his locks after each bitch—divorce—left, but who knows with any of them? After a smoke and another whiskey swig, he reached for the phone in his pocket and started to text Wife 3#.

"Look, just because I had a better lawyer than you and you got nothing, gives you no fucking right to break into MY fucking place. FUCK OFF or I'm sending the cops to your ass."

He pressed send, then scanned his backyard, wondering if someone was stalking about. Chef missed the few sets of eyes scattered in the dark before walking inside, hoping to tend to his wounds and make some fresh food for himself for a change.

He turned on the shower, and the eyes grew closer. Some red and angry, some gold, glowing with curiosity. A few sets like opals, reflecting the dim moonlight against the buzzing purple of the bug zapper just a few feet away from the backdoor. They watched the porch light dimly illuminating the small house.

The water heater was kicking on, pressure of the shower surging. He stared at himself in the mirror. Naked, bitten, bruised and bleeding. He couldn't tell what was coagulated and what was still oozing, mostly because those quick chugs of whiskey had impaired his sight and judgement. The long, hot shower had been just what he needed. It sprayed away not only the dirt and grunge from work, but the dried scabs had washed down the drain along with everything else from the day. He didn't even want to jerk off at this point. To Chef, drying off, getting into clean clothes—if he had any—then eating solid food sounded like a much better idea.

His only chair outside was a broken mess, so he sat on his bed in front of the fan, drenching his feet and legs in hydrogen peroxide. With each wince he made, he took a sip of his favorite cheap beer. Many sips later, he was sure he had cleaned each bite—wound—thoroughly and figured he'd let it all air out.

He checked his phones for messages. A few texts, but nothing from Wife #3. Three from Todd, of course, and one from Monica. *Expressing concern? Or do you need something? Fuck y'all. I'm good.* He kept wondering why in the hell they thought they needed to text him and "check" on him, but he had left abruptly—which was not like him. Chef didn't bother actually reading the texts. He knew they did—and would—need him, and he could solve all their problems tomorrow. Or the day after that, at least.

Chef limped and stumbled to the fridge. He caught a glimpse of his face in the kitchen window, but couldn't tell if it looked better or worse, especially without the bandages on. Chef tried to focus on the dirty glass showing a skewed reflection of his face. For a minute, he thought the tiny gashes started pulsating but he reverted his concentration to his stomach growling for food, any food, and not the booze he'd been feeding it for the last…twenty years.

The backdoor remained closed this time. But the sets of eyes drew not just closer, but grew in numbers as well.

He grabbed his stock pot which was dusty from lack of use. Chef rinsed it with hot water, then let it fill. His trusty cast iron pan was crusty, caked with who knows what when *slam!*

The backdoor?

"Okay, you bitch! Did you not get my text?" He limped violently to the backdoor, ready to reach for his rifle, when he stepped on something soggy, cold, and also soft. "What in the hell?" He lifted his bloodied foot and saw gray and white fur stained with brown, dark reds, and tiny little claws broken and chipped.

It was the squirrel he had obliterated from the previous night. What was left of it, anyway. He shook his leg, and the sparse yet still fluffy tail fell to the ground. Chef looked up, targeting both of the guns still against the wall. The backdoor was still closed, but he *knew* someone was fucking with him. *Gun. Phone. Phone call. Then food, because fuck this.* He called Wife #3 while loading his rifle. As the phone rang, he proceeded to scrape squirrel shit and hair off the bottom of his foot.

She didn't answer. He didn't bother leaving a message. *Maybe I'm the one who is fucking with myself. I'm drunk anyway!* The wounds on his feet and legs vibrated with pain, cratering deep into his bones. He polished off the whiskey, cracked open another beer and sliced some lemons he found in the back of his fridge.

Chef tossed the lemon scraps in the pot of water, waiting for it to boil. He made another run at dousing himself with peroxide and the ointment leftover in his first aid kit. After sitting down on his tattered couch, he really started looking at his body. When you work twelve hours a day, six days a week, and drink the rest of the time, you typically don't pay attention to much else. But this time was different. He knew his face was a disaster, his arms questionable, but his feet and all over his legs looked like...*bite marks? Claw marks?*

"I haven't had a dog in over twenty years, what the hell is this shit?"

Finally coming to the realization that this all is probably a concern, he started to poke at one of his toes. Another jagged, dried piece of skin peeled away from his flesh revealing short, wire-like hairs. Brown in color, covered by the dried blood he must have missed while in the shower.

He studied each of the abrasions and lacerations for what felt like hours. His concentration and confusion were interrupted by the water in the stock pot boiling over the rim, sizzling when it hit the flames of the gas burner. The hiss and sputter of the water took him out of his trance, and he hobbled over to the counter, looking at the fish tub containing the two lobsters.

"You ready for this, you fucks?" He picked the first one up.

It looked half-dead. There was a slight twitch in its tail, and the antennae moved just enough to let him know it was safe to throw in the water and enjoy in eight to nine minutes. He flicked one of its claws tied up rubber bands, with his own bandaged fingers, mostly just to be an asshole. Chef tossed it in the pot of roaring water. The lemons buoyed up and down at the surface while the lobster steadily sank in its jacuzzi of death, waiting for a roommate.

He grabbed its companion vigorously. This one was a bit more energetic. Its tail flapped back and forth, like it was in the jaws of death, legs wriggling like a tarantula's. Chef held it by the abdomen.

"Damn, dude! You already know your fate. While I appreciate your sass, you fucking know who has the power."

The lobster's small eyes stared right back at his. Chef swore the lobster winked at him, but before he could question anything, he threw it in the pot to be with his friend, then staggered outside for a smoke and another drink.

He ignored the squirrel bits left on the floor. Chef tucked his beer in his armpit, cigarette in mouth, and grabbed the rifle against the wall. With his free hand, he slowly opened his back door, almost expecting someone to be outside.

The bodies behind the eyes scurried out of sight the second the door opened, and though he heard something, he saw nothing. He chalked it up to the summer wind. Since the chair was broken, he sat on the second porch step, back up against the first, feet propped on the third, and stared at his feet and legs again. It was becoming difficult to focus because of the booze. The dirty light bulb illuminated the surrounding area in a cloudy, yellow haze. He took another sloppy swig, placed the rifle down next to him and checked his phone. He finally decided to text back Todd: "I left. Everything is fine. Just clean the hell up and I'll see you when we open on Monday."

Chef took another long, hard chug from his beer and another long, hard pull from his cigarette. When he was mid-exhale, the wind started to pick up. The tree branches and bushes shook violently. He gained focus through the drunkenness and the cloud of smoke he had just blown, he slowly grabbed the rifle again and aimed it at the yard.

A set of eyes. Red ones again.

He started to stand up, but the weight of his body on one leg was too much, and every single laceration on his body started to throb. Confused, figuring he was just using more muscles than he should, Chef regained his balance on both feet and concentrated on finding the raccoon, gopher, or whatever the hell it was and kill the damn thing.

Another set of eyes to his left, smaller and gold. He fired.

"I got you, you bastard!"

He ran over to the disheveled grass and dirt where he had shot the ground, apparently, and there was nothing. No blood, no leftover animal body. Nothing. At this point, he figured he should probably stop fucking around, go back inside to eat, and pass out. Shrugging, he turned around to walk back inside. When he was at the back door, he saw the eyes again. Every single set of them.

All of the mystery wounds he'd incurred the last few days pulsated, causing him to drop to the ground. He writhed in agony, grabbing at his chest, then his stomach. An odd sense of impending doom took over him while he kept eye contact with each and every "beast" staring at him from his back porch.

His skin started to tear and pucker like he was on fire. When had gained enough strength, however, he reached for his rifle and started firing at all the eyes until the magazine was empty. Between his ears ringing, his entire body burning and being eaten away, he rubbed his eyes with his sweaty, grimy hands.

Everything disappeared from the porch. He laughed uncontrollably, ignoring the fact he seemed to be slowly bleeding out. Chef crawled across the porch, opened the door from his knees and smelled something burning.

"Fuck."

The sets of eyes watched him through the screen door while he tried to pick himself up from the floor. He shuffled back and forth, leaving a trail of blood from the back door to the kitchen. Chef just knew he had to turn off the burner. He made it half-way, dropping on his side and passing out in the hallway.

The stock pot was on the kitchen floor laying in a puddle of hot water and lemon bulbs. The back door was, of course, not closed all the way.

———————————

A couple of hours later, he came to, in even more pain. He was hunched over like a tossed scarecrow in a field of nightmares. He attempted to blink and re-focus, went to rub his eyes when he realized one of his arms was weighed down with something. He couldn't feel his other arm. That sense of impending doom came back when he opened his eyes as wide as he could.

A pair of chipmunks were tearing away at his feet. One gnawing away at what little flesh he had on his left foot, the other on his right foot stuffing chunks of skin and bone into its little cheeks. Their eyes squinting, white, and glazed over like tiny sharks hungrier and hungrier with every bite of tissue they tasted.

He tried to scream, but his throat was too dry. Chef wanted to raise his arm—the one he could still feel—when he looked over and saw the gopher, a gunshot wound on its side, munching away at his elbow and bicep. It must have just started on this arm, because he could still see skin. He didn't bother looking at what was left of his other arm.

Tears poured from his eyes, some from pain and some from disbelief and utter shock. He was lying in the hallway on his back, so he turned his head as best he could. More animals—raccoons, squirrels, even old neighborhood cats were running around with glowing eyes and bloodied mouths. Some were even fighting over pieces of flesh, growling like rabid, famished creatures waiting for their next turn at him. He mustered every ounce of strength he had left, lifted his arm, and slammed the gopher up against the wall. It bit down even harder through nerves and muscle, but he managed to crush it against the wall for a second time.

This seemed to work. The neck of the gopher looked broken. Chef used what he had left of his abs to bend up his body and kick the chipmunks off his feet. He recognized that he couldn't stand, but he was able to shimmy the top half of his body around and drag himself on his one arm to the end of the hallway, attempting to fight off whatever critter came at him next.

The bleeding, the pain—it was too much. He let out a half-assed scream. If he was going to be defeated, would this really be it? He lay down on his back, making it about four feet down the hallway, close to the kitchen, adjacent to the living room. Chef was bleeding out, and most of his body became numb. His heart beat slowed, and his eyes became heavy. Fear took over the anger, but he still was not accepting defeat.

He continued to blink slower and slower, and his eyes closed. Just as he started to fade away, he felt something crawling through one of his muddied, torn-up legs. It crept from his ankle, getting to his knee. Another crawling sensation came from his other leg. Chef started to laugh, thinking this was all a dream, a drunken state. When he opens his eyes, he'll be awake in his backyard or his disheveled, empty bed.

With everything he had left, he lifted his eyelids.

Two bright-red lobsters with dead eyes sat on his chest. They dug their spider legs into his ribcage, extending their claws back and forth to tear the soggy rubber bands off. Then they finished off his face by opening it from eyeballs to ears, pinching and clawing away until there was nothing left but a crater of a man who once was.

Note from the author

A few of these stories were a work in progress for years. Most of them came to me in a dream (or nightmare) and some of them are based on real-life experiences. *Side Effects* was based on a surgery I had, being practically bed-ridden for two weeks. I pictured myself fusing with the mattress, thus came the idea for the story.

Three Eighty-Five was inspired from an apartment I lived in for one year in downtown Albany, New York. It will be forever nicknamed "The Nightmare Apartment," and yes, there were bed bugs.

Survivor and *Rooms of Terror* were inspired by what is probably the obvious—fear of dying in an elevator and anxiety. Needless to say, I hate elevators and after much research regarding modern safety mechanisms...I still avoid using them whenever possible. They're safe though...I swear.

Wolf Road is a Death Trap is based on a real road. It may not be the apocalypse yet, but driving on that street is like something out of the *Mad Max* films.

The striped, green-eyed cats are based on my cats, Spike and Zombie, who were brothers and sadly passed away in 2020 a few months apart. They were—and always will be—a part of my writing process.

About the author

With two collections of dark poetry published, Nykky Roadarmel has switched gears to her true passion—horror. Follow Nykky on Amazon and other social media platforms for the latest updates!

Nykky lives in upstate New York with her long time partner in crime (and chef) Nik, with their two cats.

The author also doesn't like writing about herself.

Cheers!

Thank you for purchasing this book

Thank you for your support! Loved it? Liked it? Hated it? Please review if you have the time.